I0590703

GUARDIANS OF MAGIC

GUARDIANS OF MAGIC

THE LEIRA CHRONICLES™ BOOK 8

MARTHA CARR

MICHAEL ANDERLE

L M B P N

DISRUPTIVE IMAGINATION

This book is a work of fiction. All of the characters, organizations, and events portrayed in this novel are either products of the author's imagination or are used fictitiously. Sometimes both.

Copyright © 2020 (as revised) Martha Carr and Michael T. Anderle
Cover Art by Jake @ J Caleb Design
http://jcalebdesign.com / jcalebdesign@gmail.com
Cover copyright © LMBPN Publishing

LMBPN Publishing supports the right to free expression and the value of copyright. The purpose of copyright is to encourage writers and artists to produce the creative works that enrich our culture.

The distribution of this book without permission is a theft of the author's intellectual property. If you would like permission to use material from the book (other than for review purposes), please contact support@lmbpn.com. Thank you for your support of the author's rights.

LMBPN Publishing
PMB 196, 2540 South Maryland Pkwy
Las Vegas, NV 89109

Version 2.01, October 2020
eBook ISBN: 978-1-64971-083-3
Print ISBN: 978-1-64971-084-0

The Oriceran Universe (and what happens within / characters / situations / worlds) are Copyright (c) 2017-2022 by Martha Carr and LMBPN Publishing.

THE GUARDIANS OF MAGIC TEAM

Thanks to the JIT Readers

Kelly O'Donnell
John Ashmore
Sarah Weir
Edward M. Rosenfeld
Peter Manis
Joshua Ahles
James Caplan
Larry Omans
Micky Cocker

If we've missed anyone, please let us know!

From Martha

To everyone who still believes in magic and all the possibilities that holds.

To all the readers who make this entire ride so much fun.

To Louie, Jackie, and so many wonderful friends who remind me all the time of what really matters and how wonderful life can be in any given moment.

And finally, a special thank you to John Nelson of the Austin, Texas Police Department who patiently answers all of my questions. I hope I made you proud. Thank you for your service.

From Michael

To Family, Friends and
Those Who Love
To Read.
May We All Enjoy Grace
To Live The Life We Are
Called.

CHAPTER ONE

The black swirl of mist seeped into hotel room 302 on the third floor of the Driskill Hotel, emerging out of thin air and swirling in the room. It gathered in inky, puffy clouds along the carpet, spreading out under the bed and around the chair. A mild stench accompanied it that was hard to place and lingered on everything it touched. The maids were getting used to the smell clinging to the room.

The temperature was quickly dropping twenty degrees as if the air conditioning was running amok. No guests were in the room.

The room was still kept empty most of the time and only used when the hotel was overbooked and desperate. Many didn't last the night and would call the front desk complaining of strange noises and a peculiar smell.

And the cold...

The worst was when they said they heard low moaning like something was trying to escape.

Today, they would have been right.

A couple visiting Austin from Indiana were happily chatting as they passed by the room.

"I can't believe that Gina Chavez. Her music was amazing! Do you have the directions to Stubbs Barbeque? I don't want to be late to the gospel brunch." The husband patted his pockets, looking back down the hall.

"Did you hear that?" The wife stopped dead in the hall, right by the door, tilting her head to listen more carefully. She pulled her sweater closer around her shoulders, hoping she'd hear something easy to explain.

"There it is again. Like somebody doing the ugly cry."

Her husband put his arm gently around her shoulders and pulled her away from the door, a cold shudder passing through him. "None of our business, dear. Let's keep going."

She moved away reluctantly, concerned about whoever was in the room.

"Sounds like someone mourning the dead. Poor thing."

"You have a good heart, Ellen. You always did."

Ellen got it half right. Lucius was a beast lost to the world in between and was crying out, determined to rip through the veil, mourning what was taken from him.

The hotel room was one of the thin places in the world where the darkness could press against the light and it was giving way to the other side. The master of the dark mist was finally ready to show himself and seek revenge.

"Rhazdon!" Lucius cried out the one name that had been on his lips for hundreds of years. A claw poked through, appearing in the room, tearing a long thin line as a darkness sucked in the light from the room. He had been keeping watch on the room, building his power. Sucking in the dark magic from lost Wizards and Elves and the occasional Gnome. He was even branching out to humans like Charlie Monaghan. The bubble that was left in the veil by Leira Berens gave him something rare in the world in between. Hope.

On the day that Mara Berens was rescued a breach was opened in room 302. Everyone filed out of the room, relieved after the rescue, not realizing the hole was never completely closed. Something had been working at clawing its way out ever since that day. Reaching out looking for power, looking for Leira Berens. He needed to find her to use her power and find his revenge.

Today was the day he finally could escape.

There was a loud rip, as if Jell-O was being scraped out of a bowl with the edge of a metal spoon, and an opening was created from the world in between. A large furry beast that was once known as a Light Elf named Lucius, stepped through the opening and onto the carpet, leaving soggy puddles with each step.

He let out a roar, opening his arms wide and balling his hands into fists as he tilted back his head, loose on the world, again.

The bellhop waiting by the elevator startled and dropped his phone in mid-text. "Shit! What the..." He glanced nervously down the hall at room 302. "Not again." He jammed the elevator button, willing it to come faster, even though all he previously knew of the room were the stories the clerk behind the counter liked to tell him. Until that moment, he was sure she was flirting with him.

He leaned over, keeping his eyes on the door and scooped up his phone as the elevator doors opened. He stepped in, biting his lower lip as another roar echoed down the hallway.

"Come on... come on... come on..." He pushed the lobby button and used his key to make sure the elevator wouldn't stop at any other floors. "I am so out of here. I'm quitting this gig hard! Rather be asking strangers if they want fries with that. At least I get to keep all my parts!"

The beast went to the window and looked out at the bright day below, watching all the people wandering around 6th Street below, going in and out of the bars and restaurants, laughing and talking loudly. "Rhazdon will pay for this. Eight hundred years. Best part, the bitch will never see it coming."

His last taste of freedom was at the height of battle as he stood by the great kings to defeat Rhazdon. He had his sword at the Atlantean's throat as he protected the old King of Oriceran. But victory was not going to be his that day. Rhazdon raised up an arm before he could plunge the steel into flesh and whispered a spell, sending a creeping darkness throughout Lucius' body. A startled look had come over his face just as he was shoved into the abyss of the world in between. The battle had raged on without him.

Lucius moved around the room feeling solid ground underneath his feet. He flexed his muscles, feeling the air on his skin. "Been far too long."

His veins pulsed black under his mottled pale skin, cursed a long time ago with powerful dark magic. It took some time, a few hundred years, but eventually he grew patient and learned how to bend all the darkness trapped in the world in between to his will. Draw it to him. Capture it and suck it dry to make it his own.

Turned out the curse had a silver lining. It possessed a magic all its own. He learned to become his own relic and even within the confines of the world in between he taught himself about the curse.

He learned how to become a shifter, turning into the beast, heightening his senses and feeling the trails of dark magic even in the world in between. He sought out the other darkness, moving more easily through the gelatinous void, eventually gaining enough power to send out energy into the world.

Lucius took a deep breath, inhaling as he lifted his chin again, focusing. The skin along his large arms rippled and the bones along his face shifted as he cried out from a familiar pain. He shook violently as his body quickly took on another form with the sound of bones cracking and reforming until a Light Elf stood in room 302 wearing full Oriceran leather battle armor, a scowl on his face.

The curse had a very dark lining to it as well. It had poisoned Lucius a long time ago until all he could see was revenge and all he felt was rage. He opened the door to the hallway and surprised a young man on the way back to his room. The man quickly slid into his room and shut the door, locking it. "South by Southwest always draws the crazies," he whispered as he stood back from the door.

Lucius drew in enough magic to fling open the door in the room next to him. He rifled through all the belongings, pulling out clothes similar to what he saw on the street below. *Somewhere in this world, Rhazdon still exists. I can feel it.* The anger pulsed in his head. Nothing was close to the right size.

He went to the next room and emptied drawers searching for clothes that would fit. Most of the guests were already out for the day, seeing the sights.

At last, Lucius found a pair of jeans and a grey sweater along with a pair of worn work boots. "These will do." He looked at his reflection and noticed his pointed ears, pulling in energy from the curse and shifting the ears into something more rounded. "That bitch is close," he growled. "I can feel it."

He shut his eyes, focusing on the distant trails of strong magic and was startled to feel something unexpected, again. The trail of bright energy emanating from Leira Berens that he had sensed even in the world in between. Stronger than anything he had ever seen in the living or the trapped. "A missed opportunity that will have to wait… for now."

Lucius left behind the jumbled hotel room and headed for the stairs. Years of watching people move around the streets of Austin had taught him something about how to blend into a crowd. "Time to go hunting," he whispered, as a thick web of inky black crept through the veins on his neck.

CHAPTER TWO

"Portasus." Turner waved his cane in the air and shimmering ribbons of green and purple floated over Harkin's body, healing the burns.

Leira looked back over her shoulder, her eyes growing wide with wonder. "My fucking mind is blown. The Aurora Borealis inside a building on the East side of Austin."

"It's a healing spell on steroids," harrumphed Turner, his eyebrows waggling. He tilted his chin down, looking up at Harkin and Correk. "A unique opportunity has presented itself and two roads appear in front of each of you." He pointed his cane at Harkin. "Tell him the truth and keep it short. No one actually cares about all the reasons you did something wrong. It's a half-assed way of saying you're sorry, not sorry. Admit what you did and stand in it."

He swung the cane in the other direction. Leira pulled away from Correk, still holding onto his hand. "And you, Correk," said Turner. "You can choose to stay angry and

7

remember what Harkin did. Most would feel that's the appropriate choice. Protect yourself from future hurt. Frankly, that's utter bullshit. You would be signing up to carry a duffel bag of shit on your back and occasionally leaning back to take a good whiff. I don't personally recommend it."

Leira arched an eyebrow and let out her first deep breath.

"What, you expected poetry?" Turner tapped the cane lightly on the concrete. "Or you can choose grace. To let it all go in one fell swoop. There will be no middle ground here." He waved his arm and shook his shaggy head, letting out a tired sigh. "But I will offer this. Instead of wondering what was lost, take a moment and wonder what could be gained. What could still be lost if you don't let go."

Correk squeezed Leira's hand and kept his breathing even, still occasionally igniting small fireballs in his other hand, letting them extinguish just as quickly. "What does letting go look like?"

"A lot like that." The Fixer nodded at Leira. "You decide what you have matters more and you start listening."

Peyton stirred on the ground, letting out a soft moan. Turner made his way to the Light Elf, getting down on one knee to take a closer look. "I've never seen anything like this. The stream of magic has been shuffled like a deck of cards." He ran his hand along Peyton's back as the large Elf's legs straightened out.

Harkin startled and tried to get closer, but Turner stopped him. "Don't fuck with a Fixer at work. I might slip and you'll find yourself covered in fur."

"So he is pissed off," muttered Leira.

Turner glanced up at her and went back to tending to Peyton. "One of the downfalls of valiantly working to fix all your mistakes by yourself is that no one else gets to add in their wisdom." Turner solidly placed his hand in the small of Peyton's back and pushed. A yellow circle of light appeared and gradually grew bigger, till it encompassed his entire body. "This should help contain his magic, for now and relieve the worst of his misery." He slowly got to his feet as Peyton began to softly snore.

Harkin stumbled over words, not sure what to do. "Thank you."

"Not necessary," said Turner. "It's what I do. It's what your son will soon be doing."

"You're the new Fixer?" asked Harkin.

"Don't sound so surprised. He's a natural." Turner brushed off the knees of his soft wool pants. "Peyton was injured years ago. Where have you been keeping him all this time? Surely, he hasn't suffered like this every day?" The anger was creeping into Turner's voice and sparks were coming out the silver top of the cane.

"I... I had him in a specially designed room."

There was a loud *crack* in the room and a wave of energy floated off Turner, undulating in a transparent wave across the room.

Leira winced from the momentary pressure in her ears. "Damn, that's what happens when you really piss off a Fixer."

"That was a basic spell," said Correk, still watching Harkin, waiting for something. "There are a lot of revenge spells in those books. Some of them had the corner of the page turned down."

"In order to know your enemy," boomed Turner, his voice echoing throughout the empty building. He took in a deep breath and let it out in a shudder, composing himself. "I'm taking Peyton with me, Harkin." He held up his hand. "There will be no arguments. I'm not asking. If you come up with a sane solution, bring it to me. Otherwise, Peyton will get the chance to live out his days in some relative peace."

Leira felt the breath catch in her throat when she saw Turner's eyes shining. She felt a ribbon of magic weave its way through her body and wind along the floor, coming alongside Turner's energy. It was the same kind of light that wanted to pull her inside of it. "How does someone love every magical that much?" she whispered. "Fuck me, he has no conditions." She closed her eyes and let herself float just on top of his energy till he poked at her, sending her backwards.

"That's enough eavesdropping, Leira." Turner cupped his hands together, whispering into them. When he opened them a morning dove flew out, circling the pair. A silver stream of sparkling light trailed the bird, weaving around Turner and Peyton. "Tell him everything Harkin. Short and sweet," shouted Turner, till the light covered them both and they were gone.

"That was mostly for show," said Correk, arching an eyebrow. He had finally stopped igniting fireballs, but a plume of steam and smoke still rose from his hand like a warning.

"I know and I appreciate it. You think you'll ever do stuff like that?"

"Give me a hundred years and then maybe…"

"Deal."

Correk looked at Leira, surprised, another piece of the anger easing inside of him.

Harkin watched the pair and felt the regret all over again, but the anger was replaced with sorrow. "I've done everything wrong," he blurted out. "I wanted to…" he stalled for a moment, muttering, "Grace," and pushed through. "I thought I could have it all. After your mother died, I buried my grief in the company of too many women."

Correk's mother. Another piece of the puzzle, thought Leira.

"Human females in particular." He chewed his bottom lip, scanning the room. "It was the first big mistake. Turner Underwood is right. I couldn't ask for help and it destroyed everything."

"What are you talking about? I didn't like what you were doing, but I never told you to leave," said Correk. He let go of Leira's hand and took a tentative step toward his father.

"You left me."

"Do you remember when it was? Just before you joined the royal court in the Light Elves' palace." Harkin gave a pained smile. "Another Light Elf… Fraekin… said I had ruined your chances at being chosen for the court. My reputation was growing."

Correk shook his head. "Wait a minute. You left to give me a chance at the royal court? That was my decision. I would have turned it down." He was shouting, his hand clenched into a fist and punctuating the air.

Leira took a step back, watching the pair. *They both want this to work.* The magic rose up through her feet, wanting to console them but she swallowed hard and pushed it back. *They have to find their own way, at least for now.*

"You would have turned it down because of me and lost your chance."

"So you took that choice from me. You keep doing that to the people you care about most."

Harkin startled, his eyes widening. "I thought it would be best," he stammered.

Correk's brow furrowed. "Fraekin. I know him. He's a good Light Elf, but he was speaking out of turn. You should have trusted the king... or changed your ways."

"I thought it was too late. And then the accident happened with Peyton."

"Injured by a Kilomea. I know all about it. It came out in your hearing."

"On the verge of death." Harkin pressed his fingertips against his forehead. "I had already lost your mother and then you."

"You walked away from me."

"I couldn't lose my best friend." His words came out more slowly. "I had this new invention that had worked on repairing a few animals from the Dark Forest. It was the first of its kind, combining technology with magic. I thought it could save him."

"You took his choices away too. You destroyed his magic and with it, his mind."

"His head is the size of a pumpkin," muttered Leira. "Sorry, that slipped out." She pressed her fingers against her mouth, her other hand on her hip.

"Leira's right," said Correk. "You left Peyton in his own

version of the world in between. They sent you to prison, and then you died." Correk choked out the last words. "Tell me why you're not a coward and a liar."

Harkin blinked a few times, curling and uncurling his hands. He looked Correk in the eye, his jaw set as the silence stretched between them.

Finally, his shoulders sagged, and the words spilled out. "I couldn't save your mother. I hurt your chances at success. I maimed my best friend."

Turner was right, thought Leira. Short and sweet.

"I was wrong," said Harkin. "I will try to do better."

Correk worked his jaw, his lips pressed together, weighing which path to take. Leira waited patiently, her hands crossed in front of her.

"I can forgive you," said Correk, haltingly. "But I don't trust you. Maybe over time I will learn how to do that. But this is the best I have for today."

"I'll take it." Harkin took a step toward Correk, but when his son stiffened, he stopped where he was. "It's a place to start. I'm not very good at asking for help."

"Fuckin A. Sorry, but that was too obvious." Leira gave a slight shrug.

"Is there anything else you need to tell me," said Correk, his arms crossed over his chest. "Now is the time to tell me."

Please don't lie to him. Leira sent up the prayer, holding her breath.

"Yes, there's a ring of mine that you possess. Do you still have it?"

Correk nodded slowly.

"Thank the moons." Relief washed over Harkin, his face

softening as the adrenaline started to leave him. "It's what Wolfstan Humphrey is after, if he can't align with me. Inside of it are my old plans. He needs them to see if he can fix his project."

"He's like the evil version of you. What? I'm not still interrupting." Leira looked from Correk to Harkin. "I thought the father and son stuff was finished. We're into the adventure now. We have something Wolfstan Humphrey wants. We can use this against him," she said, with a crooked smile. "First, we get his attention. I have an idea."

Turner Underwood jerked his head up from the lesson he was giving Leira, his eyes widening. His hands reflexively squeezed the silver handle of his cane.

"What is it? Your Fixer alert going off?" Leira was in the middle of practicing stepping into the middle of the light stream and back out again, learning to guide the energy more. She felt the tension from earlier leaving her body. "How do you do that? I don't sense anything." Leira wet a finger and held it up in the air. "There is a nice breeze coming off the lake, though."

"Something's not right."

"Is there another disturbance in the force?" Leira lifted her left knee and left arm, pushing down with her right hand. "What tai chi move is this again?" Turner was using the ancient martial art to teach Leira balance and to center herself in the middle of the light. "Part the wild horse..."

"Something's not right."

"You said that." Leira noticed the look on Turner's face and dropped her arms, tilting her head to the side. "You need to go help someone? We can cut it short."

"It's not one of our kind. At least I don't think so. Something is throwing off the balance."

"You mean, besides me for once. It's not Peyton again, is it?"

"No, he is still a magical, despite what you saw."

"I'm not sure how the whole Fixer thing works but can I help? Is that allowed?"

Turner cocked his head, listening to the vibrations of the different streams of energy that were always rolling by him from all the magical creatures in the world. Shimmering bands of different colors of light, flowing in all directions. Some of them smooth and glittering and flowing in straight lines. Others sputtering or tangling in small knots, surging ahead anyway.

He heard the low rumble of the dark, pulsing wave. "It's familiar but I can't quite place it." His brow wrinkled and he shut his eyes, leaning on his cane as he held up a hand for Leira to be quiet.

"I know this hum." He felt a tightness in his chest as the memories of the battle from eight hundred years ago came back to him, flooding him with memories. "It's not possible," he muttered.

"You're looking a little pale even for an Elf there, Turner. What the fuck is going on?"

He blinked and opened his eyes, looking at Leira. "Just thinking of an old friend of mine."

"Thinking about friends doesn't usually put a look like that on my face. Rhazdon maybe…"

"Haven't thought about him in hundreds of years." Turner looked out over the lake, softening his gaze, still focusing on the trails of magic flowing past him. He was searching for a trace of the deep, steady stream again. "Did I ever tell you that every trail of magic is like what a fingerprint is for human beings? No two are alike. They're uniquely shaped and leave energy trails that stretch around the world."

"Like their own GPS, I know. That was Correk's big clue that Harkin was still alive. I've noticed even human beings have some kind of version of them. I've used it to track killers in my old job."

"True enough. And when you have loved ones, you become familiar with that energy flow to the point where it's like hearing their voice. Some part of you never forgets."

Leira stretched her arms over her head, tempted to take a run around Turner's large estate and stretch her legs. "Has an old friend of yours come over from Oriceran? That's good news."

"That would be impossible. Besides, there's something off about the trail."

Leira stretched her arm across her chest. "Only impossible if… is your friend dead?"

"I have no idea. He disappeared during the battle against Rhazdon a very long time ago. His body was never found." Turner scratched his forehead. *There it is again.* A low rumble of magic rolled by miles away pushing other energy streams out of the way. It can't be. Turner's eyes moved back and forth as he sent out his own stream of energy to run nearby but not close enough to get entangled. Dark magic, very dark magic.

The heavy stream flashed and sent out a surge, knocking Turner's energy back into his body and throwing him backward, stumbling as he put out his arms to catch himself. Leira easily crossed the space between them and grabbed Turner by the arms, connecting momentarily with his energy as she felt the remnants of the surge.

"What the fuck was that?" Leira slowly removed her hands from Turner, still hearing the buzzing in her ears. "Okay, let me take back what I just said. Shit! No, I did not know what it was like to feel every trail of magic on the entire planet, all at once. Mind blown... Like some energy of life or something."

"An interesting way to look at it and not entirely inaccurate." Turner couldn't sense the heavy stream anymore, but the lingering doubts were staying with him.

"What was that low undercurrent. It was like some heavy, pounding backdrop to the whole thing. Not a feel good kind of groove at all."

"You could sense that?"

"Yeah, it never went away. I could have sworn it even looked up when I touched you. Like a stream of energy was looking back at me. Very creepy. Almost like the dark mist." The smile dropped from Leira's face and her jaw tensed. "What's going on? What do you know?"

"Not as much as I thought, apparently. More will be revealed but hopefully, we'll see whatever it is coming."

CHAPTER THREE

L eira sat down at her desk across from Hagan. "Explain it to me again. Slowly this time." Leira took a bite of the Mexican Hot Chocolate doughnut as Hagan glanced down at the familiar pink box. "Doughnut after…" She pulled the box closer to her.

"You say that like I have no self-control." Hagan sat down and slapped his hands on his desk. "I have plenty… there's always more doughnuts where these came from." Hagan laced his fingers together and pursed his lips.

"You're ruining a very good doughnut experience for me. Tell me already." Leira put down the doughnut and brushed her hands, giving Hagan the dead fish look.

"Okay, good… Fine… Now I'm ready." He winced, trying to find the right words. "Look, I think it's time I hang back from the big operations." He waved his hands around at the large open space. "Back you up from here and work on more local cases that involve fewer dark forces that can reach out and throw us around like rag dolls." Hagan took out the white cotton handkerchief he always had at the ready in his back pocket and wiped his forehead.

Leira didn't say anything even as her eyebrows went up. She picked up her coffee and slowly took a sip, not taking her eyes off Hagan.

"You're dickin' me around right now, aren't you? Nice, Berens. Look, I'll say it. That last battle took a little something out of me. Hell, I think I was dead for a few second there. And I have this whole thing going with Rose that I like to call a good life. Oh, for pity's sake, Berens, say something!"

"What kind of asshat do you think I am? Like I'd say no, we started this together, we end it together? Geez, Hagan. Besides, the next big baddie looks like it might be the worst." Leira gave him a crooked smile as she took another sip of coffee. "Of course, this means I'll have to heckle you over an earpiece. Best part of the job."

Hagan let out the breath he was holding and mopped his face again. "Well... that goes without saying. Hell, maybe I'll turn out to be more use as tactical behind the scenes. You know, I was a little worried you might be..."

"That's a long way around the barn to say I'm selfish, you know." Leira got up from her desk and walked around to Hagan. "You put in your time, Hagan, and you've stood beside me at more than one battle. You get to call it when it's enough. Good for you."

"What's this? Are you about to hug me? Don't do that, Berens. Oh geez. Partners don't hug. It's in every manual."

Leira stopped short and patted him on the back. "Best partner I could ever have. Thank you, Hagan. I mean it... for everything."

"Okay, well, then... eat your doughnut." Hagan swallowed hard and changed the subject. "Hey, you think Yumfuck would hang out here at the office occasionally."

"If you put in cable and more snacks you have a shot."

"Where is he, anyway?"

"I don't ask myself those kinds of questions anymore. He's got an entire side gig going. Something about Batfuck..."

Hagan let out a snort of laughter. "Seems he's joined the family business. Hey, I heard about the good news. A wedding... you'll have to figure out how to throw a bridal shower. What a year you've had, Berens."

"Yeah, a little bit of everything. Reconstituted an entire family, even a dad and found out my relatives didn't come from Ireland after all. Even Correk found his father."

"Yeah, Harkin. How did that go? Not as simple, I'll bet."

"More fireballs, less swearing, and still ongoing. All wrapped up with a few run ins with some dark mist no one can really explain." Leira felt the edge of something. "Mom is over the moon. I'm happy for her," she said, distracted.

Hagan let out a small belch, patting his belly as he reached into the Voodoo doughnuts pink box. "You're gonna have to work on the whole being happy thing. Your demeanor lacks a certain something."

"Have the feeling I'm missing a pretty important clue. Can't quite put my magic finger on it."

"You will... you always do."

Leira shook her head to clear it. "Hey, remember your motto. There's always more. Might want to slow down just a little. You're not retiring just yet. I'll still need you just as much backing me up here while I'm out there chasing bogeymen. We're just ramping things up."

"Berens that's the nicest thing you could have said to me," said Hagan, chomping down on a Maple Old Fashioned.

CHAPTER FOUR

The young Wizard, Toby Wheeler, stood in the field wearing a silver reflective vest, directing the cars in the late afternoon sun with a flashlight to make sure no one headed for the deeper part of the pasture and tore up the good Kentucky grasslands.

Toby kicked a piece of sod with the toe of his sneaker, still frustrated that he was so far away from the action. "Nothing more than a glorified orange cone." A white Volvo station wagon parked at the end of a line and a well-dressed middle-aged couple got out, ignoring Toby and heading toward the gravel road that led to the manor in the distance.

Toby held up both hands, giving them a double dose of the middle finger, dancing his hands back and forth. He eyed his wand in his pocket and slid it out, holding it lightly in his hand. "So tempting…"

Using a wand would have been easier but the possibility of prying eyes was too big, and it was impressed upon him not to break the laws. Toby was well aware of the consequences of crossing his new employers.

After all, he was the nephew of one of the oldest ruling families, making him a kind of nobility. But his mother had run away from them all as a teenager and turned her back on the lineage, choosing instead to ignore the dark magic and marry a Wizard serving the Silver Griffins. The worst kind of betrayal.

The moment Toby turned eighteen he decided to rectify that mistake and ran right back to the old families, expecting a warm embrace. Instead, he was met with wary looks and given menial assignments. Still, it was better than the future he had back home with his parents. College and then off to the cubicle life. No magic in there at all.

"Hey, kid!" An overly-muscled Wizard with a buzz cut to hide the lack of hair and wearing an ill-fitting navy-blue sport coat stood impatiently at the edge of the road gesturing to Toby with his meaty hand to follow him. He was one of the regular muscle that hung around the family at the ready when muscle was more appropriate than magic.

Toby startled and dropped his wand into the grass, scrambling to pick it up. "Damn! What an amateur. Drop my own wand." He picked it up and wiped it off across his pants leaving a damp splotch.

He was still muttering as he slid the wand into his pocket and eagerly followed the Wizard down the path, jogging to keep up with the man. "I wasn't... I mean... I would never use my wand. I mean, not without orders..." The words sputtered out of Toby and he could feel the sweat under his thin cotton shirt. The chill in the air of an early spring Kentucky cold front was making it worse and the vest was no protection against much of anything.

"Forget about it, kid. Not my department. Although, word to the wise. Don't move a muscle unless someone tells you which muscle and how to use it. If you fuck up badly enough it won't matter who you're related to." The Wizard tapped a thin, jagged purple scar along his chin. "I speak from experience." He gave a smile that was angry more than anything else. "A certain kind of loyalty is expected around these parts."

"What kind of loyalty is that?" Toby was still walking fast just to keep up with the Wizard's long strides.

"Absolute. Keep your head down when you get in there and just listen. Think of all of this as a kind of schooling and you just might survive."

Toby swallowed hard. *Survive. That is hard core.*

They walked the rest of the way in silence, as Toby did his best to regain his composure and match the stony demeanor of the bulky Wizard.

The Wizard looked over at Toby just as they got to the stone steps leading up to the tall wooden doors and he let out a snort. "You're too skinny and young to pull off that mug. Save menacing for another day. How about you go for invisible and do your best to fade into the background and just watch. Remember what I told you. Observe everything. Participate in nothing, no matter what you hear. Not a gasp, not a chuckle and under no circumstances if you like that geeky look you've got going and want to keep it, do you say anything. Got it?"

Toby nodded hard and snapped his mouth shut, taking a deep breath and headed up the steps.

"Lose the vest, kid. You're not parking cars now."

Toby quickly slid out of the vest and dropped it by the door as the Wizard pushed open the heavy wooden doors that were brought over from an old castle in Romania. Toby's uncle thought they added a certain ambience to the whole effect.

They passed quickly through the front hall and down a short hallway that curved to the right to a far wing of the house. They entered the great ballroom just as the doors were being closed and the Wizard turned and gave Toby a sturdy shove toward a far wall where other lackeys and servants were standing quietly. Their eyes were all focused on the long, wide wooden table set up in the center where the heads of all the old families were already seated. At the end of the long table sat an older Wizard with wavy silver hair and a long, straight nose that looked like it could touch the top of his full lips. He was wearing a jet-black suit and black tie against a white shirt. At the cuffs were silver wolves and on his hand was a large signet ring bearing two wolves making the infinity sign.

Hanging overhead were different woven banners with the various family crests representing the old wizarding families of dark magic since they first came together thousands of years ago and formed an alliance.

"Hey..." Toby gave a nod to the young Witch standing closest to him. She looked at him long enough to give him a withering look and flick her long, brown braid off her shoulder. "Okay..." Toby put his hands behind his back and stood up straighter as he looked around the room.

The Wizard who escorted him into the room was standing against the far wall with other Witches and

Wizards and Toby quickly caught on to a certain hierarchy in the room that started with the most powerful sitting at the table and gradually went around the room till it stopped squarely at the crowd where Toby was standing. Toby let out a defeated sigh, garnering a few looks from the young Witches and Wizards right around him. He looked across the room and noticed the beefy Wizard staring at him and straightened back up, determined to get this right. You can do this, Toby. *Hell, you belong at that table! Be the observer... be the observer...*

Sirius Pickering lifted his hand and a silence fell over the room. He raised his wand high over his head. "Extemporius." The sound of water pouring down could be heard from outside the walls.

Every head turned toward him as he lowered his hand and let out a deep breath, waiting. "The time has come to push back against the Silver Griffins," he finally said. A spell had been cast so that his deep baritone easily filled the room as he rested his hands on the table. "The time has come to make our presence known to the human population."

A small murmur of voices went around the room but harsh looks from others quickly silenced them. Toby watched eagerly, pressing his lips together, determined to make a good impression or at best, no impression at all.

"It's time we used our newest talent to persuade others that we are not passive players anymore and it would be in their best interests to bring us to the bargaining table."

"We should not have to bargain with anyone!" Agnes, an older witch with long, blonde hair that was caught up in a neat low bun slammed her fist onto the table. Toby shook and wanted to let out a gasp but was too afraid. He dug his nails into his palms and watched, eyes wide to see what would happen next.

Sirius was breathing harder, his chest rising and falling but he did nothing to silence the Witch. "We have everything we need to gain the advantage. The beasts are ready! Time will not always be on our side. If we wait till magic begins its return to Earth…" she shook her head, "it may not be as easy as it is right now, especially with the intruder."

"Do not mention Wolfstan Humphrey to me. He is only a complication. Focus on our real adversaries. Have you forgotten who sat in this seat not too long ago? Your own brother served this council for over twenty years before he was swallowed by that dark menace." Sirius' voice was gradually getting louder till it was booming and echoing off the walls. "To this day we still do not know what that was that ate his essence and absorbed his magic from the inside out." Sirius raised his fist in the air, shaking it with fury. "His body still walks among us but none of us can say he still exists in any realm or what the hell took him from us!" The crystals in the chandelier over their heads shook gently making a tinkling noise as the banners swayed.

An older witch with long, jet black hair hanging straight down her back took a sip of tea from a pale pink bone china cup, gently setting it down. Juliana Pickering looked unruffled by any of the drama. "Sirius, my darling, Agnes makes a valid request." She arched a carefully manicured black eyebrow. The only sign of impatience was the gentle tapping of her red nail against the fragile china cup. "We have managed to get the mortality rate down to a respectable fifty percent and have created enough shifters under our power to at least make a statement."

"Not enough of them to stop an army. Not enough of them to rip Wolfstan Humphrey apart."

"We don't need that, my dear. We just need enough of a demonstration to let everyone know what we're capable of doing. Let their own fears come up with the rest."

A young Wizard with dark hair, slicked back against his scalp spoke up. Toby recognized his older cousin, Emerick. "Are we certain that these new shifters will obey us once they're out in the field? They may just run off, back to their families or worse, not survive even a skirmish."

"Don't doubt your mother, dear. It's not a good look for you."

"None of them will return to their families," said Sirius. "They're too afraid of their new powers and ripping their own flesh and blood to pieces." Sirius let out a deep throated laugh. "I expect we would lose some in a fight, but we'd learn from the experiment. Perhaps you are right, Juliana, as ever."

Agnes frowned at being overlooked but held her silence. No one at the table ever pressed a point but so far for fear of the consequences.

"These are strange times we're in. Even the suggestion of magic returning is upsetting the balance of power that we have quietly enjoyed all these years." Sirius sat forward in his high-backed upholstered chair. His face grew sour as he spoke. "We are being challenged from every side and it's not in our nature to sit back and quietly take it. Humphrey is creating his own army and he doesn't see anyone as his ally. The Silver Griffins would tie our hands and at one point, we might have listened..."

Toby saw his uncle glance over at him, but he stared back blankly. The Wizard across the way gave him a nod of respect.

"But some dark mist is hunting our kind." Sirius looked over everyone's heads at the table, off into the distance. "My oldest friend is a bag of flesh for some unknown host and two other Wizards and a Witch have disappeared without a trace. Even some of our younger ones, teenagers, have gone missing."

"You still haven't mentioned our greatest enemy."

Sirius snapped his head around, anger returning to him. He raised his wand and shoved Juliana's chair backward away from the table, surprising everyone.

"Do not test me. Not even you. I'm well aware of the bitch that is out there, growing stronger all the time."

Juliana stayed where she was, saying in a low growl, "Say her name."

"I'm not afraid of her. This mongrel who's part Elf, part human and even has some trace of Witch in her. She surrounds herself with amateurs. We have defeated worse!"

"Say... her... name..."

"Leira Berens! Leira fucking Berens!" He shook his fist as the banners swayed overhead.

Juliana looked up at the Witches and Wizards ringing the large room standing near the tall windows. "Learn this name and get to know your enemy." Her voice was low and icy.

"She holds the fucking light inside of her and is

learning to bend the very essence of magic to her will," said Agnes.

Juliana shrugged, not bothering to look at Agnes. "Leira Berens is one very young being against thousands of years of a strong alliance and a new army of shifters. Hell, Wolfstan Humphrey may even distract her just enough. The next steps may not be easy, but we are used to struggle. We will get what is ours, in the end. The bitch is only another obstacle in a long line of them and like all that have come before her, she will not survive what's coming."

"You sound sure of yourself."

"Well, of course Sirius. That dark mist that hunts us, hunts her as well. It even seems drawn to her and to that same light. We will meet her in battle but perhaps we can draw the darkness there too and just get out of the way."

CHAPTER FIVE

Mara stepped into the White Horse bar on Comal Street and waited for her eyes to adjust. She knew better than to pull in any magic and break the bar rules. The place was jammed with pool tables to one side, poker tables in the middle and seating pushed to the walls.

"There you are," she said, smiling and held out her arms wide to hug Turner Underwood. He was already sitting at the bar, sipping two fingers of bourbon, neat. "Farrelly was telling me about his boy, Jenkins."

The bartender grunted and gave a nod to Mara. He was a Crystal, disguised with a glamour but the spell didn't go far enough to hide the frigid air right around him. He was the air conditioner for the entire bar.

Standing next to him was an eight year old boy, half Crystal and half human. He was wearing a white apron folded over to accommodate his smaller stature, but he was already approaching his father's shoulder. Farrelly put his arm around his boy's shoulder and pulled him close, giving him a proud shake. "He's just like his old man," he said with a grin.

"What'll it be, Mara? Long time since you've been in here. Heard about your troubles. Glad to see you got out. Worse than Trevilsom," he said with a shake. He shook a finger in the air, squeezing one eye shut. "As I recall, you loved a gin and soda." He poured a healthy amount of gin in a glass, not waiting for Mara to answer, and gave it a shot of soda water.

"Very good memory. Sure, it's early in the morning, but okay," she said, eyeing Turner's drink. The Fixer tapped the top of the bar and slid his glass across. Farrelly refilled it in one practiced motion. "Thanks Farrelly," said Mara, "and nice to meet you Jenkins."

Farrelly held the gin and soda near his son and gave him a nudge. "Watch this," he said with pride. The young magical smiled and blew on the bottom of the glass, frosting the bottom. "Huh? Yeah? Pretty good," said Farrelly, putting down the glass in front of Mara and patting his son on the back.

Mara smiled and got out a dollar, pushing it across the bar to the boy. "Clever."

"We'll leave you to it," said Farrelly. "The Fixer doesn't generally come in here just to shoot the breeze," he said with a wink. "Come on Jenkins."

Mara watched them head into the kitchen with a shake of her head. "Imagine the lust a human would need to get close enough to a Crystal to procreate. What does any Crystal know how to do that would make it worth the frostbite?"

"You'd be surprised," said Turner, arching an eyebrow.

"Really… Respect," she said with a chuckle. "Thank you for rescuing those refugees."

"Right to business. Something I've always admired about you. You know, I've known all along about your passageway."

"Then you knew I was in the world in between."

"I suspected but I didn't have proof and I had no solution if you were. Best not to pick at that wound. Little did I know that your granddaughter was so special. I'm sorry it took me so long to see it."

"It had to come to the surface."

Turner took a long sip of his drink. "I suppose we have Correk to thank for that."

"He does seem to be teaching her a thing or two." The two old friends both laughed.

"Are you going back to your old life, Mara? Rejoining the underground?" Turner made a temple with his fingertips, resting his hands on the bar.

"No, that's my old path. I want something different. A new challenge, especially since everyone around me is pairing off and going on to their own adventures."

"I have a proposition for you. I've been approached by the humans in charge of this country to start a school. A boarding school on my property in Charlottesville, Virginia. A place to teach magicals and encourage them to serve the government."

"You're on board with that? Sounds like the feds using kids to grow their own friendlies."

"Only encourage. It's needed. There are only a handful of magical schools around the country and with the gates gradually opening, maybe we should teach getting along with our human hosts." He drained the last of his glass.

"With you in charge, I know it will retain the right mission and do some good."

"When do you need an answer?"

"As soon as possible. The school needs organizing and there are already parents interested in sending their students. Hell, there's a gargoyle Correk dropped off. Something will have to be done about that. Then there's the dorms being built."

"Sounds like a lot of work."

"It will be, but there's also a large staff. You'll oversee everything. I'm calling it, The School of Necessary Magic. Kind of catchy, don't you think? What do you say?"

"I'll think about it. It may be just what I'm looking for."

Leira stood outside the Arab Coffee on 24th Street waiting for Correk to catch up with her. "What was that about?" She called to him as she watched the morning sky lighten against a slate grey sky. *Love a good Texas morning.*

Correk ran the short distance across the street, crowded on all sides by clusters of students from University of Texas, streaming back and forth across the nearby campus. "A Witch had her phone snatched. I managed to retrieve it for her." A young woman smiled up at Correk and gave him a long look from head to toe as she passed by.

Leira gave Correk a crooked smile. "Sometimes I forget about that Elven charm and then that happens."

"Not always Elven charm. That was a young Light Elf. Sometimes, they just like me."

Leira elbowed Correk as she started to walk faster down the street. "Sure, big guy. It's all you."

"Hey, I thought we were going in that shop back there?"

"That hookah shop, not hardly. That's not where the magical mystery tours start in these parts. Way too on the nose. The general population would notice if too many average looking middle-aged people kept going in and out. Probably think it was a drug stop. I would have in my old job."

"Then where are we going where no one would notice?"

"There…" Leira pointed to the Starbucks still a block away. "Our way to get to Chicago and this time without the long drive. That coffee shop is like the magical community's version of a bus stop. Finally, an answer to why we needed a Starbucks every few blocks. I have it on good authority the whole thing is owned by a Wizarding family. Apparently, Seattle is a hub for that kind of thing."

"I'm surprised I didn't know more about this. I know everything about the kemanas and the cities."

Leira looked both ways and didn't see any cars coming as she scooted across against the light with Correk in tow behind her. "Lacey said the transit system is hush, hush. Those are her exact words. It's more vulnerable to sabotage and too many dark players are out there. The whole thing is covered in spells and there are absolutely no humans allowed. They can't even touch anything without going poof!" Leira threw her hands up in the air as they got to the door of the Starbucks.

"Poof… you know, we could make all of this simpler and take a portal. I've learned a few new things from Turner's books."

"No portals on Earth. It's too risky, especially when there's something cool that will get us there in just about the same amount of time without the threat of eternally hanging in Jello. Oooh, I'm getting coffee before we head out."

"Get me that lemon cake and a grande cappuccino with a half shot of caramel and soy milk."

Leira turned around and gave him a pained look. "How do you even know all of that? I'm getting you black coffee and you can add cream if you want. Okay, the lemon cake as well but only because we're hitting the road." The line moved forward quickly. "I thought I'd miss Hagan more but it's like having his soul mate along with me. I appreciate that the Universe saw fit to fill the void."

"What'll it be?" A frazzled young woman looked up as Correk leaned in and said quickly, "a grande cappuccino with a half shot of caramel and soy milk and a piece of that lemon cake."

Leira gave them both a dead fish look. "A large black coffee for me."

"Name?"

"Correk."

"Are you paying for it too?" Leira pulled out her wallet from her purse and dug around for her credit card.

They went and waited with the crowd of students and people on their way to work, easily blending in with the crowd around them.

"Check out the beings around us..." whispered Correk, leaning toward Leira.

"Your breath smells faintly of burnt Cheetos. You eating your feelings today?"

"I know you're dying to ask about Harkin."

"A little. Any progress?"

"We've agreed to meet at where he's been staying." He glanced at Leira. "In a lab set up in the Dark Forest."

"That's a twist I didn't see coming. Did Perrom know?"

"I don't know. I haven't had a chance to ask him yet."

"Let me know if you want me to go with you." She patted his chest. "You packing junk food? What is that?"

Correk pulled out a small spell book to show her. "Latest homework. I ate the last of my junk food supply looking through one of these spell books. Accidentally started a small fire in Turner's trash can. Minor issue. Nothing important was harmed. Take a better look around." He gave Leira a nudge as she let the smallest amount of magic flow through her and saw the energy light up, dotting the crowd all around her. It was an even mix. A Wood Elf right next to her sensed Leira's energy and gave her a wink. "How you doin?"

Leira frowned and shook her head but before she could answer a young man in a green apron came and set two cups down with a slice of cake wrapped in wax paper.

"Core Ick? Your order's up."

Leira slid through the crowd, stepping in front of a large woman with a feather boa around her neck and a backpack full of books. Leira saw the tip of a pecan wood wand poking out between her books.

"Core Ick?" asked the young man. "Cool name. Sounds like a band."

Leira pressed her lips together and grabbed the coffee, handing Correk's cup back to him, with the cake balanced on top of the lid. "Thanks," she said, taking

MARTHA CARR & MICHAEL ANDERLE

Correk by the arm and leading him toward the restrooms.

"Please tell me the entrance isn't in the bathroom. We're not getting flushed down something? If you say yes, I'm opening a portal and leaving without you." Correk slipped the wrapped cake in his pocket and sipped the hot cappuccino as he looked around for another door.

"I can see we dipped into the Harry Potter of it all somewhere in your past. This isn't a fairytale, and no one gets flushed. If you'd relax, you'd see where we're going." Leira took a deep breath as the cement block wall at the end of the narrow hall became wavy lines and a woman standing by the ladies room door looked right through them, no longer able to see them as a spritz of chocolate filled the air.

Leira pulled Correk toward the wall just beyond the bathrooms and kept walking without pausing, heading right into the wall. Correk suddenly got a strong whiff of chocolate as they slipped through to the other side. "Not at all what I expected the bathrooms to smell like. Not bad…"

Leira rolled her eyes as she pulled him through. "There's a glamour there that keeps out the humans. Feels like a solid wall to them. It even puts out a mist that erases what they see or hear by the bathrooms, so no one's ever seen vanishing into thin air. Probably for the best by a bathroom where everyone's drinking coffee."

"That smell of chocolate." Correk looked around at the cavernous opening and the commuters hustling to get to different parts of the globe. Different Elves, Witches and Gnomes rushed past him clutching children's hands or briefcases or shopping bags as they climbed stairs to even higher tracks or descended down a maze of stairs into the depths below.

In the distance were another set of stairs heading in every direction with lines of commuters heading up the stairs to a different Starbucks just a few blocks away, always near a train or bus line.

Leira took a sidelong glance at Correk, giving him a crooked smile. "You know, for once it's kind of nice to see you in awe at anything magical. I didn't even know that was possible. You're having a time with magic this week, aren't you? Blowing things up, setting things on fire and finding out there was still a lot left to learn."

Correk's head was tilted back and he was looking up at the artificial blue sky and clouds passing overhead giving everything a much cheerier facade. "Reminds me of the post office back home." He turned around and was startled to see a stand selling newspapers, magazines and candy in an alcove where the Starbucks had been on the other side.

"Yeah, I don't get that whole time and space thing with that one, either," said Leira. "I've just decided to let some of this go for now. Maybe one of Turner's books will explain it to you. Come on, these steps take a while and you're in the way." Leira pulled Correk toward the staircase as more commuters continued to come in and stream around them, some of them giving Leira a dirty look or a loud 'tsk' as they hurried on to their destination.

They fell into line behind a tall, lanky Wizard who was wearing pants that left his ankles bare and a jacket that ended just before his wrists. They went down two twisting flights as the Wizard made a left turn and headed off in another direction and they found themselves behind a small Gnome woman wearing purple Crocs and jeans, carrying a large HEB shopping bag, muttering to herself the entire way.

"If I don't get home by lunchtime, I won't get the roast in the oven on time. If that doesn't happen dinner won't start on time and then the presentation will have to wait. Oh, bother. Maybe if I take the number two line, I'll get home a little faster. But then I'll have to walk a few extra blocks. Of course, I could use just a teensy amount of magic and move the roast along a little faster. Who would know? What's the harm?" The small Gnome realized she was talking too loud about using magic and looked up suspiciously to see who was around her, smiling at Correk even as she continued to nimbly descend the stairs. They all got to a juncture with a sign pointing to the right that had a large red two on it and another pointing to the left with a blue B on it. The Gnome hesitated but only for a moment before rushing off to the right.

Leira took Correk by the hand and pulled him further down the stairs.

"How do you know your way so well?" He looked over the edge at the open space on every side of the stairs. "What is holding up everything?" Everywhere he looked were different staircases and walkways humming with activity but no signs of a berm or a wall or even a beam stretching into the darkness.

"Full of questions. Lacey Trader gave me a map. Those other routes are headed to other places," Leira said over her shoulder. "Some of them cross oceans and go under mountains." Leira was easily taking the stairs, keeping in time with the other fast-moving commuters. "All of it was created the last time the gates were open and kept hidden all this time. Look, there's where we're headed."

At the bottom was a string of rail cars all polished and shiny with the number 58 painted in gold on the side, shimmering and vibrating. They took the remaining steps down as Leira hurried toward the rail car and grabbed the last seat, holding a place for Correk. Commuters crowded in until even the aisles were packed.

"Do you mind?" A short, round older Gnome with a brushy brown moustache rested his briefcase by Correk's feet and pulled out his hat and gloves, putting them on. "Might as well get ready," he said, smiling.

Correk leaned toward Leira. "Tell me again why we needed to meet with Lacey in person and a phone call wouldn't do?"

"I would have preferred that too. Mom's bridal shower is tomorrow and there are a few things left to do. But Lacey Trader thinks there may be traitors among the ranks. She's not sure but she wonders if someone is feeding the old families bits of information. Everyone is related to everyone else somehow, anyway. The old families have filtered into a lot of places over the years."

"Like the phones, I take it."

"Or worse and would it be that hard to use a little magic to listen in when you wanted to? Lacey has made it a new policy that she won't say anything outside of the walls of the Silver Griffins headquarters where the spells can ward off eavesdroppers." Leira leaned forward to get a better look at the Gnome whose face was level with Correk's. The Gnome gave Leira a nod and held onto the pole as the train gave off a loud thrust of steam and started moving forward, pressing Leira back against the seat. Everyone in the aisles braced themselves and leaned against the poles or the seats, familiar with the lurch. All of it was a routine part of their day.

"How the rail cars work is another mystery to me since there's no engine as far as I can tell." Leira looked out the windows on the side at the landscape passing by in a blur.

"This entire rail car is an artifact, I imagine, or running off a crystal from a nearby kemana or both." Correk leaned as far as he could toward Leira, turning away from the Gnome.

"You think anyone knows you're the new Fixer?" whispered Leira. "It's like you're a celebrity in these parts."

"No, I don't and today's not the day to tell them. Let me figure out how to do a tenth of the spells in those books without leaving burn marks and then I can hand out business cards."

"Very old school of you. Pretty sure the native population does that over their phones now. You think they get reception down here?"

The rail car started to slow as everyone leaned forward and steam surrounded the car.

"That was no time at all. Not sure I like it as much. No reason to bring along snacks." Correk waited for some of the passengers in the aisle to move out before he stood up.

Leira followed him out, easily falling in line again with the commuters. "Granted, not much of a road trip. Come on, we have another hike up the stairs."

The lines of commuters heading up the stairs moved along at a steady pace as an Elf waved to a friend heading down the stairs, a delighted smile on her face. "Kerry!

Kerry, hi! What are the odds?" she shouted. Kerry looked up and waved a mittened hand back, even as she continued down the stairs.

Magicals peeled off at different levels, heading to catch a different rail car or to come up at a different Starbucks as Leira and Correk continued to climb.

Close to the top Leira watched a Wizard in a puffy jacket deftly reach into the back pocket of a balding Wizard in a green coat right in front of him, sliding out a wallet with two fingers. Leira pushed the Witch in front of her gently to the side and pushed her way to the Wizard, tightly grabbing him by the elbow. Correk wound his way up just behind her.

Feels good to grab a petty thief for once. She squeezed his arm hard enough to get a squeal as he dropped the wallet.

"Hey, that's mine!" The balding Wizard reached down to retrieve his wallet as the entire, snaking line came to a halt and everyone leaned over the sides to get a better look at what was slowing down their ascent. Correk heard the grumbling behind him and turned around to give a cold, hard stare to the offenders who quickly looked away. *This is not going to go like Leira thinks it will.* He looked at the turned faces. *But they understand. A short stay in Trevilsom.*

"You and I are going to become fast friends," said Leira, keeping her grip on the man's arm.

"No need," said an older, round Witch in glasses who appeared by her side, pushing her way through the crowd. "I'll take it from here." The Witch showed her badge with two silver-colored circles intertwined as the thief's face became ashen. "You were warned, Boris. Come on." Stairs just to the right began to light up as the Witch made her way with Boris, pulling him out of the crowd.

"Okay, now I'm not sure I did the right thing." Leira watched the two disappear into the distance as everyone commenced climbing the stairs again.

"The Silver Griffins don't brook with any kind of criminal behavior, but they'll be fair."

"I'm not sure we'd define fair the same way."

"You're probably right. They've never been known for just giving someone a ticket."

"Come on, we're at our destination," said Leira, still looking back.

Correk took Leira by the elbow, steering her away from some grumbling commuters. At the top they were met by a Witch who walked them through a different exit from everyone flowing around them and Leira felt the same pull through the darkness as it gradually gave way to the light and she was back in the same paneled room.

Correk watched Leira step through the passageway before stepping back and making his way through the Starbucks and out to the street where he saw the Witch dragging a wilted Boris toward a minivan for transport. The cold spring Chicago wind whipped at his face.

"No time like the present to try out a spell," he muttered. "Luci tenebras. Dimittas." Correk's eyes glowed momentarily as he bent his thumb and forefinger into a square. Fog seeped out of the ground filling the air on one side of the street. The Witch looked back startled to realize she wasn't holding anything anymore and Boris was nowhere in sight. The witch removed her glasses, wiping off the dampness from the sudden fog, peering into the gray cloud. "Well of all the…"

Correk led Boris away from the fog, toward the Red Line stop, pulling him out of the isolated fog. "You get what I'm guessing is a fifth or sixth chance, Boris. Don't waste it. Call this number if you want to stay out of trouble and find real work. They'll help you." Correk pressed a card into Boris' palm with the number of a network Turner Underwood created a long time ago to help magical beings.

He gave Boris a shove toward the subway stairs. "Hurry…" Boris hesitated, his mouth open and clutching the card but he got his wits about him and took off at a run. Correk turned and walked back into the thick fog as it parted to either side for him and he easily found his way back to the Starbucks. He paused at the back wall, letting himself relax and watched the wall dissolve and the scent of chocolate filled the air. He walked through and took a sharp left toward the door Leira went through and opened it, looking into the darkness. "I suppose this is what Turner meant. Be the calm. Rule number one of being a Fixer." He stepped forward, enveloped by the darkness as the door shut behind him. *Be the calm.* His mind drifted back to Leira.

CHAPTER SIX

"And this is the cafeteria." Lily Sharpton stood back, excited, lacing her fingers together. "Oh, Gloria, this is my Aunt Lois. She's visiting and stopped by to see where I work. Well, some of it anyway. I wish I could take you up to my lab, but it's only employees and only those with certain clearance." She glanced nervously at Gloria as she passed.

Lois smiled at her niece. "It's okay, I completely understand." She leaned in and whispered. "After all, the Silver Griffins are big on security too." She stepped back and winked as Lily's face warmed.

"Aunt Lois we can't even whisper about m-a-g-i-c around here," she said softly.

"I'm pretty sure humans have learned how to spell." She batted her hand. "Of course, no worries. No more wand talk."

Lily blanched, biting her bottom lip. "And this is the lobby," she sputtered. "Oh! Over there is the private entrance. That's where all the bigwigs come and go. Of course I've never actually seen it," she added quickly, smiling sheepishly at a group heading for the elevator. "Hello Valerie. Just showing my Aunt Lois the public areas. Just the public areas." She gave a small wave and took her Aunt by the elbow, steering her away from the traffic of people near the bank of elevators.

Lois tilted her head to one side and smiled. "How many times have you snuck in the private entrance?"

"Only a few and no one saw me. I used the cloaking spell. Worked like a charm."

"I trained you well." She gave her niece a tight hug. "You get back to work."

"Yeah, I better. I'm close to a breakthrough," she said, excitement returning to her voice.

Lois kept the bright smile on her face and gave a short clap. "Well done! I'm not surprised."

"Lily, you coming?" A young woman leaned out of the elevator, one hand on the opening.

Lily glanced quickly at her watch. "Oh, yeah, I'm coming. Where'd the time go?" She quickly squeezed Lois' hand and started walking backward to the elevator, even as her friend kept waving her arm. "Well, this is where I leave you, Aunt Lois. Just leave your visitor's badge with the guard and pass through the security gate and back out to the parking lot."

"You'd better go. I think I can find my way out of the building."

"Okay, okay, I'm coming. What? Right. Of course, it's right there. Make sure you look at all the flowers on the way to your car. It's really cool how they spell out Fleeker."

"I'll be sure to do that." She waved and smiled till Lily

was on the elevator and the doors slid shut. Then she pulled off her visitor's badge and left it in a nearby potted plant, whispering, "Occultatum," with one hand on her wand under her jacket.

A breeze blew through the lobby, blowing dust into everyone's eyes and swirling around Lois till she was hidden from view. She pulled out her wand and waved it at the door to the private entrance till it gave a faint click and she could slip inside. On the other side of the door was the narrow elevator door and the hallway to the private entrance.

She blew on the tip of her wand and waved it at the elevator doors. The smell of metal burning filled the air as a smile grew across Lois' face. "There. Patsy, you would be so proud of me right now. Just one picture." She slipped out her phone and snapped a picture. Across the elevator doors, burned deeply into the metal was the message, *We're coming for you.*

Lois let out a trill and headed for the private exit, stopping with delight at the sight of the dark SUV parked in the space marked *CEO*. "Nice repair job," she muttered, feeling the side panel. She blew on the end of her wand again and carefully wrote, *Aloha motherfucker*, laughing all the way to her car, the end of her wand still smoking. "It really is a useful greeting. Can be taken so many ways." Her phone buzzed and she answered it. "Hello granddaughter, yeah it's done and no complications. Part one of your plan is complete. Oh, glad I could help. Yes, I made sure it would get his attention. Trust me, he'll know we got through his security."

Correk emerged into the light of Lacey's office just as Leira was turning around to go back for him. She recognized the look on his face. It was the same one Hagan gave her every time he needed her to have his back and ask questions later. Leira turned back and rested her hands on her hips, as Correk came and stood by her side.

Turner Underwood was waiting for them, sitting in a brown leather upholstered wingback chair. It was brought in from another room especially for him. Age has its privileges. Lacey was sitting behind her desk, a plate of cookies between the two of them.

"Coffee is coming," said Lacey. "Have a seat. We can get started. Everyone knows each other here so we can skip the formalities. There's no time these days, anyway for all the niceties. The wizarding families had a meeting that was mandatory attendance. All the old lines were there, of course. The consequences of being a no-show make the Silver Griffins look mild-mannered."

Leira gave a sidelong glance to Correk as she took a mug of coffee from the Witch who came into the room carrying a tray.

Turner lifted his shaggy head, his hands resting on his cane and cleared his throat before speaking. "It was quite the performance... I hear. Fortunately, we have a few spies of our own who are willing to serve the greater good. Or at least the side that isn't interested in pummeling humanity into submission. But we needed you both here for a reason." Turner looked at Leira with a patient, kind smile.

Leira sat back in the hard wooden chair, her hands

wrapped around the mug, the bracelet sliding down her wrist. *This isn't going to be good.*

"Their star attraction for the meetup wasn't even invited." Turner tapped his cane softly against the floor. "That would be you, Leira. Your name and face were taught to every attendee. They see you as their greatest threat to securing their power. Even more than Wolfstan Humphrey."

"Not to sound braggy but that's not news, exactly. That Wizard who got dragged to the other side... he's one of their own, isn't he?"

"He was the head of the entire network. Their leader of many years and thought to be invincible... till you."

"He must have told the families about me. He already had a bee in his bonnet about me before the world in between made him its bitch. How does this change things?"

"It's all about focus and intent, my dear." Lacey waved away the Witch coming in to see if anyone wanted more coffee. "Please see that we're not disturbed." Lacey waited till the door was shut with a soft click. "The old wizarding families are wealthy and powerful and have been around for centuries. Their kind are everywhere. You've run into them without knowing it but before they didn't know it either. That may be changing and in this instance that gives them an advantage. Stay aware of your surroundings. Keep the troll by your side a little more often."

Correk shifted in his seat. "Was that the only item on their agenda?"

Leira knew what they were going to say before they even said it.

"I know you see what Wolfstan Humphrey is doing as

the greater evil. You may unfortunately prove to be right. But the families' plans are the more immediate emergency. Their experiments with turning humans into shifters has been successful enough." Lacey pressed her lips together in disgust. "They're ready to move forward with the next part of their plan."

"What's the rest of the plan?" asked Correk.

Turner interrupted her, shaking his head. "We don't know what that means, exactly. Only the leaders sitting at the table got the details, but we can surmise a few things. We expect them to use the shifters in soft spots heavily crowded with people to put the fear of magic into human beings and get them to pull back."

"General Anderson will never do that. Hell, the entire U.S. government will never do that. They'll push back harder with bigger weapons." Leira leaned forward in her chair. "That would play right into Wolfstan Humphrey's hands. He's already building alliances with corporations."

Turner raised his eyebrows and could feel the weight of nearly a thousand years. "True enough. We start with the more immediate and engineer our way back to Mr. Humphrey. It may be the only way."

"Deal with the shifters first," said Leira.

Turner slapped his hand down on the arm of his chair. "It's difficult to know where to aim a weapon if you can't locate the enemy."

"Shifters have an advantage…" said Correk.

Leira sat back against the chair. "They can change back and blend into the general population. Fuck, they're still human even if they've been modified."

Turner pointed a finger in the air. "This is where you

come in handy, Leira and why they fear you so much. Your ability to ride the energy without having to physically be there lets you follow the trails that these shifters will leave behind. If you can use the light, bend it without becoming part of it, you can trace the shifters and identify them."

"Maybe… It's not quite that simple. The energy doesn't always show me everything or maybe it can't. It's more like puzzle pieces at times."

"More than we have right now."

Correk sat on the edge of his seat. "Surely we can track them before harm is caused."

"Until they release them outside of their current confines there is no trail to follow." Turner sounded weary. "We will have to play a waiting game and hope the damage is not too extensive."

I can find some of them. Leira ran her fingers along the bracelet. *There's a connection there. I can feel it.* She looked up at Correk. "We'll be ready." It was all she said. *Better to keep this growing connection to myself, for now. No need to give false hope.*

CHAPTER SEVEN

Correk and Leira emerged in the Starbucks just before lunchtime. The place was filled mostly with students working on term papers, and writers trying to finish their novels. Correk pulled Leira out the side door of the Starbucks and held onto her hand as they headed down the side street and into the alley.

"What are you doing? Did you see something?" Leira peered out from the alley, ready to pull in energy if it was needed.

"No, I wanted to talk to you. Although, it's good to see you're taking Turner's warning seriously. We need to find the troll and keep him closer."

"We needed an alley for you to tell me that? Come on, we need to get to the warehouse and see if we can figure out where the shifters are being kept."

"Not the warehouse." Correk held onto Leira's arm. "We need to figure out a different plan. The warehouse is a government facility designed to help the human population. All well and good, but this may be something that we can solve without alarming them, or worse. It's only incidental if something good comes out of it for the magical beings on this planet." Correk shook his head, his face tense. "They will not take any of this well and once they know, it will be out of our hands. Self-preservation will kick in and General Anderson will come up with his own strategy."

Leira looked at his hand still on her arm, but let it go. They had come a long way in such a short amount of time. "Lois has been warning us about this from the very beginning. It's a good bet tampering with humans and their DNA is the line that crosses into panic land for the government."

"We make it a rule to meet at the sanctuary. Not the one on Oriceran, we'll use the one outside Austin or even the one in Alaska or Hawaii when we need to. No one outside of who we choose to invite will even know of the meetings. And we keep that number small."

"Not a bad idea. There's so many sides to this puzzle now and the sanctuary will keep us hidden from everyone."

"From Wolfstan Humphrey."

"Did you secure the ring?"

"I'm keeping it with me for now. Turner Underwood offered one of his safes but Wolfstan Humphrey has been able to get into almost anywhere. Correk formed a ball of light between his hands, singing into it and pulling his hands apart as the opening grew. "Now we need to convince the Gardener of the Dark Forest it's a good idea."

"Shouldn't be hard once he finds out we're going out on our own, at least to hunt the shifters and find the old Wizarding families."

"And he owes us," said Correk. "He knew all this time my father was alive."

"He may not see it that way." Leira stepped through the opening into the forests at the edge of the sanctuary as Correk followed behind her. Leira always liked to take a moment and take in the calm. No sounds of technology or people rushing somewhere.

"I do love this place. It's like I can breathe here without staying aware of who's on my six all the time."

There was a rustle from the edge of the forest. Leira turned, expecting to see an animal foraging nearby. Instead, a familiar figure stretched his arms over his head making the trees and bushes appear to bend and roll.

"Perrom! You're here." Correk smiled and took the last few steps at a fast clip, grasping his good friend's hand.

"I hate it when my father's right."

Perrom emerged from the green foliage, the scales along his skin flipping over from different shades of green to honey brown. "He said it wouldn't be long before you two showed up here again. He predicted the divides would become wider and you'd have to choose sides. I take it things have gotten worse."

"Not worse as much as we are coming to understand the new reality," said Leira.

"Come on, follow me further into the woods. Even with the magical protection over this land, these days more caution is necessary. I don't want to find out the hard way that the darker forces have figured out a way to infiltrate the spells."

"The Gardener wouldn't be very happy."

"He would start his own war if the wrong element ever

penetrated a sanctuary. He's the last guardian of so many things."

Leira stopped on the mossy path. "Well, that brings me to our request, and this is probably far enough in, just in case it's a hard no. We need a regular place to meet and share information, plan our next steps." She looked all around at the dense forest, the light dappling the leaves. "The sanctuaries are the best places I can think of where we can talk openly."

A macaw landed easily on Correk's shoulder, only managing a raised eyebrow out of the Light Elf. The colorful bird let out a squawk, spreading its wing as it side-stepped down his shoulder to Correk's outstretched arm, scooting right back up his shoulder again. "The world is changing. Magic is slowly seeping back onto Earth and thanks to Rhazdon everyone got an early heads up. Being able to meet here will be the thing that helps keep the sanctuaries safe."

"Damn, that's two in a row. The old man has powers beyond what he's even shown me." Perrom smiled, his pupils coming together to look straight ahead. "He already had the same idea and told me to wait till you showed up and asked. Said you'd appreciate his generosity more." The smile faded as he reached out to a deer who ventured close enough to nibble on nearby leaves. "He won't tell me what else he sees coming or if it's his best guess or some strange ability he had that he's kept to himself. Either one is possible, but I can tell you that he doesn't like whatever he believes is coming next. Too many powerful rivalries breaking out into the open for their share of power in whatever form they can get it." He hesitated, fading into the background and reappearing again. "It's why he's been helping Harkin. The research may become necessary to counter Fleeker."

"The Gardener didn't know that when he decided to shelter my father."

"You're right. It may just have been about friendship."

Correk cleared his throat. "That I can understand, I suppose."

Perrom rubbed the fur along the deer's back as the deer pulled closer, nuzzling his side.

Leira watched, amazed, as Perrom's hand took on the look and feel of the fur he was rubbing, the texture spreading up his arm. "We will protect the sanctuaries with our lives, if necessary. We will be guardians of the magic here and not let the forces out there destroy it. Anyone who comes to a sanctuary will understand that they do so with the same agreement."

"Agreed," said Correk, holding out his hand. Perrom put his on top as they waited for Leira to do the same.

"What, this is a thing on Oriceran too? Do you guys fist bump and hide away in man caves?" Leira put her hand on the top.

"What's a man cave? Humans don't live in caves anymore."

Correk let out an annoyed sigh. "You both are taking the cool factor right out of this. Come on, this is marking something sacred. The beginning of our Forest of Solitude."

Leira let out a snort as the bird squawked at her from Correk's shoulder. "Birds of all kinds generally like me," he said.

"Yeah, well Super Elf, that's not a bad name for it. Okay, what do we say here? This is getting weird."

"All for one…" said Perrom.

"And one for all!"

"Our two worlds are more aligned than people realize." Leira flexed her fingers, feeling the tired muscle of a nearby bionic animal. *We are going to need Harkin.* She could feel it slowly settling down to rest. "Too bad coming together is turning out to be a shit show so far."

"Not everything is written yet. Things change quickly these days. We may make a difference yet." Correk held out his arm for the bird.

The macaw spread its wings, pushing down as it took flight, rising above the canopy and letting out another loud squawk before disappearing from view.

"We should be going. Till we meet again, my friend."

Perrom startled at Correk's words and started to say something but stopped himself. *I should tell him about Ossonia. We're old friends…*

Leira watched the bird fly away, feeling a momentary peace. *May it last.* She felt the magic stir in her feet, a thin sliver of it riding up her spine, responding to her emotions. The skin along her chest was flushed as she breathed harder. "The bionic animals are nearby." The words slipped out. *Fuck, broke Hagan's rule. Said too much.*

Correk wasn't even subtle about it. He reached out and grabbed Leira's arm, letting the energy flow through him as the bracelet jangled on her wrist. "The connection is growing. You can sense when they're around." He looked her up and down, feeling some of the same connection. "If one of those animals is killed…"

"I will feel their pain, but I won't die." *I hope...* "And it seems to have a limit to the distance. I can't feel anything if they're not close enough. Close like, within a mile... or two."

"That's why the magic sought out that shifter." Correk was putting two and two together pretty quickly. He searched her face to see if she was trying to keep something from him. "You suspect the same thing, don't you?" His stomach turned sour as Leira gave a hard nod.

"I didn't know for sure. There was no point in making a pronouncement with no field testing."

"Field testing?" His voice rose to a shout as Perrom took a step back and the branches above rustled with the sounds of animals and birds moving further away. The deer Perrom had been petting spooked and ran quickly through the woods as other deer poked their heads out to get an idea of the danger and quickly followed suit.

"From the first damn day I was ordered to help you, you drilled it into me how important it was for two beings who work together to trust each other and tell each other everything. No fucking secrets! I believe those were your exact words."

"Ordered to help me." Leira's expression was strained and anger was quickly replacing the sense of peace. *That didn't take fucking long but it's leaving in a way I didn't expect. Less weaponry but still hurts.* "That's the first thought on your mind."

"I think this is not my fight so..." Perrom turned to go but no one else seemed to notice as Correk cut him off, still shouting, waving his arm.

"After everything we've been through that's where you go. Do you trust me or not?"

Perrom glanced back over his shoulder at his friend as he muttered, "He has got it bad... Elf bad. Last a thousand years bad... Good for him, poor bastard." He smiled as he slipped further into the forest, the scales along his skin flipping to match his surroundings. He could still hear the shouting as he blended into the background, whistling to the songbirds nearby, any guilt about Ossonia floating away.

"Fuck me, of course I trust you! But... I didn't want..."

"Didn't want what? There are no half measures with trust. You're either all in or you're playing games."

"I didn't want to see you hurt again." The words came out in an angry rush. The image of Correk lying on the battlefield close to death flashed in her mind. She stood there defiant, her hands on her hips, determined to win this one.

Correk shook his head. "Enough."

"Enough what?" She raised her chin, waiting. "I would have told..."

Correk grabbed Leira by the opening to her leather jacket, pulling her close and pressing his mouth eagerly against hers, letting his tongue glide against her teeth. Leira stiffened at first, her arms out to the side but she quickly gave in and wrapped her arms around his waist, gently biting his lower lip.

The energy swept up through her feet swirling inside of her and rushing from Leira to Correk, sweeping around them, lighting up their corner of the forest, sending a beacon into the sky. Perrom was already a distance away and saw the light pushing through the thick canopy. "Now that's interesting. Good for you, my oldest friend."

Harkin ducked his head out from the river, a sprite resting on his shoulder. Water poured off his head as he looked and saw the light high above the trees. He felt the tug of familial energy.

"Oh, a heart connection," said the sprite, her wings fluttering.

Harkin felt some of the pain ease from his shoulders and he let himself smile, just a little, as he slipped back beneath the surface. An unfamiliar feeling swept over him. *Hope.*

Leira pulled back from Correk looking at his face and resting her hand against his cheek. "This is not the best timing," she said, as the light continued to swirl around them. "We still have a few assholes to go take care of."

"If this is your unique way of saying you're all in, I'll take it."

Leira let out a short laugh and rested her head against his chest for a moment. She let out a deep breath as the peace returned to her and she pulled back, the light dying down and the magic swirling in reverse, back into the ground. "That was a badass kiss, Super Elf," she whispered, her hand still on his chest. "Really does kind of make opening day of your Forest of Solitude kind of special. You've had a big week."

He reached down and gently kissed her again.

"We need to go." Leira slowly stepped back from him. "We need to..." she let out a deep breath... "fuck, stick to the singleness of purpose here." She held up her hand. "Making out with you is not it. Not yet anyway. We have to go save the fucking world first. Then we figure out what this means." Leira headed out of the forest before her good intentions faded away, the rush of energy making her feel lightheaded and her heart beating a little faster.

Correk caught up with her easily, pushing aside a branch. "That's right, Eireka was sent away when you were still pretty young. I was grown when Harkin pulled his vanishing act. I can explain it to you if you like. Even show you in more detail. What do they call it on this planet? The birds and the bees."

"Very funny. How long have you been wanting to do that? I wasn't the only one holding back bits of pertinent information."

"Hit me in the moment. Hey, now that we have a place to meet, we should form our own Magic League."

"You really have to make more friends here than just the troll. You sound like you hang out in a comic book shop all day. I think Yumfuck actually has more friends than you do."

They came out into the open field at the edge of the forest. The day was a bright blue with a light Texas wind rustling the long grass.

"I'd hold your hand, but I know you well enough to know you'd rather run down a felon."

"Oh, dear God, you suppose right. Now you're just messing with me. Where's a good gun battle when you need one?"

Correk let out a snort of laughter and formed a ball of light in his hands, singing into it as he pulled it apart, creating a portal that opened up into her living room.

"Feeling cocky, opening portals to go such a short

distance," said Leira, stepping through into her living room.

At the last moment, she reached back and held out her hand for Correk, giving him a crooked smile. He took her hand tightly and stepped through, back into the guest house.

"You two look a little too happy." Mara sat up on the edge of the couch, cocking an eyebrow as she tilted her head. "Good day?"

Leira startled, squeezing Correk's hand as she let it go. "Nana... what are you doing here?"

"We have to finish planning your mother's bridal shower, remember? Mayhem can take a back seat for a moment. And whatever you two are up to. Don't bother protesting. It's about fucking time. I thought I was going to have to sit you both down."

"Well, Leira could use a few pointers on..."

Leira jabbed him hard in the ribs with her elbow as Correk shrugged. "Just trying to help."

"At last, a little happiness in this house. Protect it like a precious flame, you two. There are forces that will test it... Now, come help me pick out a theme for this shindig."

"A perfect example of my life right now. A little bit of world-wide threat mixed in with normal life stuff." Leira sat down next to Mara as Correk waved at them, heading out the door to the bar for a beer with Estelle. She smiled at him as he waved, still feeling his lips against hers. *Damn, that was good.*

CHAPTER EIGHT

Yumfuck set out from the guest house with his small Ninja Turtle backpack early in the morning in search of a mission. He had found his new calling and was even making a difference. Tucked into his backpack was his mask and cape. "Time to get back out there. I am Batfuck..." he growled as he slid under the gate and headed out into the world looking for trouble.

He made his way down Rainey Street keeping an eye out for a chance to test his skills again, but the street was mostly empty except for the few people stopping in the food truck court further down the block getting a breakfast taco before they headed for work. The troll easily slipped around their feet without being noticed, breathing in the odor of bacon and egg wrapped in a tortilla. "Yum...." He stopped and looked back, wondering if there was time but held up his little paw. "No..." The troll shook his head as two college students working off a hangover walked by.

"Extra salsa is the key. It gets your blood going," said the young man in shorts, flip flops and a UT sweatshirt.

"I don't know…" said his friend in baggy jeans and a button-down shirt. His hair was rumpled and there were dark circles under his eyes.

"You need to do something, Ralph. You look like death warmed over."

Ralph grimaced, hesitating.

"Come on! Do it!"

The troll watched, licking his lips. "I can see how Ralph got himself into trouble last night," he squeaked.

"You hear something?"

"Quit delaying. Take a bite. A big one. There you go. That's how you do it."

Ralph chomped down on the side of the taco, splintering the shell as Yumfuck slid underneath, his mouth wide open ready to catch all the falling pieces. He opened and shut his mouth, chewing as fast as he could while bits of cheese, bacon and egg and bits of tortilla with globs of salsa rained down. Tiny sounds of gargling erupted out of him. Ralph peered over the taco he was eating and saw the small troll with green hair wearing a tiny backpack and jumped, dropping the rest of the taco.

Yumfuck easily caught it gently in his arms and ran for the security of the nearby bushes.

"You see that? There was a…a…a gerbil wearing a backpack! He stole my taco!"

"Oh Ralph, this is worse than I thought. Dude, you're still drunk! Come on, we'll get you a taco with some of that ghost pepper salsa. That'll knock it right out of you. Come on, you'll thank me later."

"No, wait... but..." Ralph spied the troll devouring his taco, shoving pieces into his mouth. Yumfuck always liked to be hospitable and waved, smiling, his cheeks bulging. "Yumfuck!" he chirped, happy with the way the day was starting. "Maybe just one more." He trilled, adjusting his backpack and pulling out his mask, tying it around his head. "Go in undercover, motherfuckers!"

He crept along the rim of the grassy food court till he got to the first truck. From there it was easy to creep along the back of each truck till he got to the short green truck with large pink hearts and the words *Taco Baby* painted at the top. There was a long line crowded in front and the young woman in a white t-shirt and stained white apron was moving fast, taking down orders and grabbing the tacos being made behind her.

Yumfuck scrambled up the side of one of the large tires positioned right under the order window and perched himself on the edge, leaning out. A flutter of white napkins landed on top of him and a tall, leggy blonde woman with a long braid looked underneath. "A troll," she whispered, delighted. "In a mask, no less!" She put her finger to her lips and smiled, giving the troll a wink. "I've got you." She stood back up and pulled out two extra dollars. "Can I get one more?" She took the warm taco wrapped in foil and bent down, handing it over to the troll. "Not a rescue, okay? My mom would kill me if I bonded with one of you."

The troll let out a cackle and grabbed onto the taco with both hands, lifting it over his head as he slid off the side of the tire. Ralph watched the bobbing taco run toward him through the grass and felt the remains of what

MARTHA CARR & MICHAEL ANDERLE

he just ate bubble up inside of him. "I am never drinking again... This time I mean it!"

"Aloha motherfucker!" chirped the troll as he ran across Ralph's foot.

"Tell me you saw that! Tell me you saw the taco talk! Clear as day! Aloha motherfucker!" Ralph held out his foot as if it were evidence of something.

The young woman whispered into Ralph's ear too quietly for anyone to hear. "Never was, never will be." Ralph teetered, rocking back on his heels and fell backward into his friend's arms, out cold. "You are a serious lightweight, dude," his friend, muttered, laying him out in the grass and splashing his face with water.

The girl watched the troll disappear around the corner and smiled, grateful for the little reminder of another home.

Ralph sputtered and opened his eyes, looking around. "What happened?" His face turned red as he saw all the people gathered around him.

"Dude, you were insisting the whole world was coming to life and talking to you. Dancing gerbils, talking tacos! What exactly did you drink last night?"

Hands reached out to help Ralph to his feet as he looked around dazed. "What? Last thing I remember was paying for the parking. Did we eat yet?"

The girl slipped out of the park, turning just in time to see a taco in silver foil bobbing further down the street.

The troll found an old twisted root to sit on under a bush and took off his mask, laying it on top of his backpack. He opened the foil, diving headfirst into the center of the taco, his mouth wide open. "Mmmm... yumfuck." He wiped his mouth on nearby leaves and balled up the foil, making a nice layup into the nearby trash can, then scrambling out from under the bushes and heading toward Davis Street. Ralph's friend shook his head hard. "Dude... did you just see? Never mind. Think we got hold of some bad tequila last night. Now I'm seeing things."

Yumfuck put his mask back on, pulling out the cape to complete the disguise. He made his way down Davis toward the frontage road by the highway, determined to find someone to help. He rubbed his belly, letting out a loud belch, tasting the taco again and smiling. "What?" He held his paw up to his pointy ear, listening. There it was again.

The sound of loud mewing was coming from a nearby pecan tree growing in front of a strip mall. An orange tabby was stuck in the tree near the top, too frightened to come back down the way it got up there, crying for help, tucked into a corner by the trunk.

"At last!" The troll swung into action, flexing his tiny muscles for a moment, getting into character. Yumfuck adjusted the mask and set out to climb the tree, digging in with his claws as he got closer to the cat. The tabby saw the masked troll coming closer and mewed louder, backing away from the approaching new superhero. Yumfuck stopped on a lower branch and trilled, calming the cat, studying the best way to get her to safety. He took off the mask and cape, putting them away and set the backpack aside, hanging it off a narrow branch. Still trilling, he grew to the size of a large dog, bending the branch he was standing on as he reached up to grab the cat and put her under his arm.

The cat looked at the rows of sharp teeth and tufts of green hair on the growing furry troll in front of her and she arched her back, hissing. The troll was not deterred. "Batfuck does not back down!" He reached out for the cat, scaring her as she rolled backward off the branch, half falling, half leaping from branch to branch till she was finally back on the ground. She shook all over, her fur still standing on end and scampered away.

The troll watched from the tree, only a little disappointed. "The cat was rescued, still counts." He shrunk back down to his usual five inches and gathered his backpack and mask, scrambling back down the tree. Once safely on the ground again he brushed his hands together. "All in all, a damn fine morning!"

CHAPTER NINE

F raekin sat down heavily on his favorite stone bench in the royal gardens. It was his favorite place in the entire kingdom and usually quiet with very few magicals. The sky was a particular blue and he watched, amused as he hummed a familiar tune and the flowers swayed in time with him. "A perfect life, all in all."

He was getting older, even in Elven years, his long flowing hair a stark white and the occasional ache in his bones on cold mornings. *Nothing a good spell can't still fix.*

He found himself taking more breaks in the day lately, carving out minutes to notice the flowers or read a good book. He opened the dark blue book in his lap and watched as the words appeared on the yellowing page. A history of Oriceran and in particular the Light Elves played out, starting with the Great War over seven hundred years ago.

Fraekin had read the book several times, once holding on to it a little too long and watching it sail through the air when the Gnomes reclaimed it. It was his favorite story and not just because of his own father's bravery in defending the king, even if it didn't end well. The king had disappeared in the end.

Fraekin shuddered and not for the first time. "Lost to the world in between," he muttered. "Death would have been better." The elderly Light Elf startled at the sound of a deep chuckle. Grey shadows circled him quickly, blotting out the sky and his surroundings till he couldn't see anything in the dense fog.

"I'm glad you see the benefits of death," whispered a disembodied voice. A face briefly flashed in front of him, but he didn't recognize the magical. The end came quickly with a slash across the throat as Wolfstan Humphrey shouted, "Harkin lives!"

He disappeared into the shadows just as quickly as he appeared, the haunting laugh lingering in the air. *That will teach Harkin to start a fight with me.*

The book in Fraekin's hands dropped onto the ground, alerting the Gnomes a book was being mistreated and it was quickly retrieved, flying around the castle and through an open window into the hands of a waiting Gnome. The red poppy on his black bowler celebrated with a triumphant wet raspberry.

"Hmph, a stain." The Gnome held the book closer, peering at the deep red stain. "Blood…" He looked up at the Gnome closest to him and back at the book, bringing it closer and taking a long sniff. "Yes, blood. Take this book and keep it safe. Sound the alarm. Something has happened."

The Gnome quickly retraced the steps of the book, easily following its flight path and found Fraekin slumped over on the bench, the life force drained out of him. Others came running from the castle, hanging unseen in the sky, tripping down bronze stairs that were rapidly appearing from every window.

"Make room!" Queen Saria made her way through the middle of the crowd, the vines on her crown turning a darker shade of green at the sight of Fraekin's lifeless body. Her chest rose and fell with anger as she snapped her fingers, fiery symbols appearing along her arms.

The images of Fraekin's last moments appeared suddenly in front of her, her anger rising as she watched the delighted smile on Fraekin's lips interrupted by a grey cloud shrouding everything. "Damn shadow magic," she hissed. But her eyes grew wide when she heard the last words before the images faded. "Harkin lives!" rang out causing a rippled gasp among the crowd.

The Queen's lips curled with anger and she gritted her teeth, curling her fist. "Harkin," she hissed. "Not again! I thought we had dealt with you."

There was yellow tape across room 302 at the Driskill Hotel as most of the management met downstairs to decide what to do about the room. There was a suggestion to play up the haunted features of the room and see if there were any takers but most of the staff wanted to lock the door and never open it again.

Several guests complained of finding their belongings ransacked and a strange clear goo clinging to everything. Dry cleaning was quickly offered and a free night but no real explanation beyond a shrug and mutterings about how strange people are these days.

A junior manager was sent up with a bellhop to inspect the room and write down any of the damage for the insurance claim. Both young men stood nervously outside the door, debating about going inside.

"We have to at least inspect the room." The junior manager grasped the iPad close to his chest against his dark blue polyester jacket with large gold buttons.

"I say we make a good estimate of the damage. No one else is willing to go in there. They'll never know. Put down that the carpet's ruined along with the bedspread, and maybe the curtain and a lamp. I'll bet we're close to being right."

"No, that's too much of a guess. Look, we can compromise. We open the door and stand right here and see if we can tell what's ruined. Then at least if they ask us if we saw the damage we can answer honestly."

"What if they ask if we went in the room?"

"We'll put a foot over the line so we can answer that one too." The junior manager reached out, hesitantly touching the doorknob, prepared for anything.

"Gaaah!" The bellhop let out a yelp, startling the junior manager who jumped back, plastering himself against the far wall.

"What the hell did you do that for?" His voice came out in a squeak, breaking in the middle.

"You almost peed yourself, didn't you?" The bellhop grinned, cracking his knuckles. "Okay, I'm ready now. Do it! Let's light this rocket!"

"You do it, you little fucker!"

"I'm pretty sure the hotel employee manual says you can't talk to me like that."

"Do it or I'll throw you in the room myself and shut the door!"

"Are you crying? Fine, I'll do it. Geez, you should be thanking me." The bellhop wiped his damp palms on his pants, swallowing hard. "I broke the tension," he muttered, leaning back as he touched the handle with the tips of his fingers.

"You have to use the key card, you dolt."

The bellhop let out a frustrated sigh. "You could have mentioned that. That means we're even." He held out his hand for the card as the junior manager slapped it into his open palm. "Okay, attempt number two."

"How is this number two? You didn't even have the key card the first time!"

The bellhop rolled his eyes, pressing his lips together to keep himself from saying what he was really thinking. *What a knob. I hope whatever's in here eats him. Then, I'll apply for his job. This could turn into a really good day.*

He inserted the card, pulling it back out again as the green light flickered and he turned the handle, touching it as little as possible. He pushed the door open, holding it there with his foot as the junior manager leaned down and pushed a rubber wedge into the bottom of the door.

"There, now we can get a really good look." He smiled as he looked at his handiwork, pleased that he had thought to bring it with him.

The bellhop's mouth hung open as he stared into the room. Bubbling was appearing in the middle of the hotel room at his eye level as if the fabric of the air was overheating or some horrible transparent rash was developing and clinging to the atmosphere. The bubbling spread, making it hard for him to see the window behind it, and bulged toward the two men. "Do... do you...do you see that too?"

"What now? Is this another one of your... Holy crap!" The junior manager looked up annoyed, in time to see an arm push through the bubbling, sticky film.

"You almost expect someone to yell out bubble, bubble, toil and trouble," muttered the bellhop. He reached out and clutched the junior manager's sleeve.

A muscled shoulder appeared as the hand reached out further, looking for something to hold onto to pull itself out of the world in between. The head emerged of the old King of Oriceran, still in battle gear and full leather armor from his battle with Rhazdon outside the old castle eight hundred years ago. His long silver hair was tied back with a thin strip of leather. He yelled out, bellowing as his other arm emerged and he ripped the veil between the two worlds, stepping into room 302 of the Driskill Hotel, towering over the two men still cowering by the door, frozen to the spot with shock and fear.

"We should run."

"Yeah, we should run. That's a very good idea."

Neither one of them could take their eyes off the tall Elven king in leather armor still holding onto his sword. "Where is this hell hole?" bellowed the king as he looked around at the thick carpet and paisley pattern on the quilted bedspread.

"Austin?" chirped the bellhop.

The junior manager swallowed hard and finally stood

up straighter. "I'll have you know this is one of the finest hotels in town!"

The old king lifted his sword over his head as the two men gasped and clung to each other, backing up to the far wall in the hallway.

The king swiveled and wielded his sword, slashing at something trying to claw its way out of the world in between as a black mist puffed and a thick stench hung in the room. More grey arms appeared in the rip, the flesh hanging off their bones and long claws slicing at the air. "I need fire! Bring me a torch!" The king slashed left and right as limbs flew into the air, turning into puffs of black mist as more arms came up to replace them.

The bellhop ran his hands frantically over his jacket trying to remember where he left his Zippo lighter, finally finding it in his pants pocket. He got it out, lighting the small flame and leaned toward the king, taking a few steps into the room. "Here," he said, his hand shaking.

The junior manager slapped his hand on his cheek. "Are you fucking kidding me? That's going to do the trick?" The color had drained from his face, but he couldn't bring himself to move off the spot where he stood.

The king turned, grabbing the lighter and held it close to the bubbling from the world in between, catching it on fire as it sizzled and popped. Cries of anguish erupted from the world in between as the opening burned and the veil sealed itself. The fire burned itself out, tar dripping onto the carpet quickly burning a round hole everywhere it spilled.

The king turned, slashes along his arms and sheathed

his sword. "I'm in search of a beast that escaped from the world in between. Can either of you help me?"

The junior manager's eyes rolled into the back of his head as he teetered back and slid down the wall out cold.

The king looked to the bellhop as he curled his hands into fists just under his chin, keeping his elbows pressed against his body. "A... a beast? Um, there was a report of something weird a day or two ago," he stammered. "What are you?" The bellhop waved his hand in the direction of the king's pointed ears. "Fucking Warcraft or something? That is the most badass special effect I've ever seen! How the hell did you do that?"

"I'm the King of Oriceran in search of the beast that controls the dark mist." The king stepped forward, the ground shaking under his footsteps.

"Okay, cool... staying in character. I can dig it. You guys ever use extras?"

"Never was, never will be..." Turner Underwood got to the doorway as the bellhop froze in place. "Come on, we don't have much time, your highness. The spell doesn't last but a few minutes. Welcome to Earth."

"Earth? Have the gates opened again? It can't be that long since I fell into that abyss. Who are you?"

Turner doffed his hat and bowed. "I am your old friend, Turner Underwood, although unlike you, I have aged quite a bit, and no, it's only been about eight hundred years. Long enough."

"Turner," gasped the king. "You've gotten older my friend." The king clapped Turner on the shoulder as Turner walked toward the stairs.

"I brought you some clothes that should fit. You can

change in the stairwell. It's good to see you again too, your majesty. I thought you were lost to us forever."

"I recognize that room. The world in between opened up there before, didn't it?"

"Yes, and you fought bravely alongside your grandson, Prince Rolim." Turner led the king quickly down the hallway and to the stairs, holding open the door. "We should hurry. This city puts up with a lot, but this may test their love of the weird."

"The beast has escaped from the world in between. We have to find him before it's too late."

"We will, but first let's get to a more secure location. A reunion is in order."

"You don't understand… The beast, he's a friend. Lucius is alive."

Turner's face paled as he hesitated and shook his head. "Even more reason to hurry. The old way of doing things is changing with every day even as our pasts are coming back to haunt us."

CHAPTER TEN

Correk stopped at the edge of the treeline, taking in the outline of the building tucked so cleverly in the depths of the Dark Forest. He waited, taking in the sounds of monkeys running along the branches overhead and birds calling out to each other. His longbow rested against his back.

"He already knows you're here." The Gardener let the scales on his body turn back to their deep brown color as he emerged from the shadows of the forest. "There's an alarm system that warns of anyone magical or human approaching the lab. Although it's rare for someone to survive a walk through the Dark Forest."

"I've often wondered how much of that tragedy was designed by you." Correk didn't take his eyes off the building, swallowing hard.

"It's more accurate to say, I don't interfere."

"Unless someone threatens the animals."

"This is their home. They deserve to be left in peace. You can set your bow aside. He's unarmed, except for his magic. Go in and talk to him. Get as many answers as exist or you can handle."

Correk turned to say something to the Gardener but he was already gone, blending back into his forest. Correk could track the Gardener's direction by listening to the animals' sudden movements. A trick Perrom had taught him a long time ago.

He shook his arms and let out the breath he was holding and started walking. "Time to get some answers."

He pushed the door open and stepped inside, taking in the sparse surroundings and the quiet. There was a long table along a wall with scattered electronic parts and different tools. Under a row of windows that had vines growing around the frames were bigger pieces of machinery in different states of disassemble. Correk glanced toward an open door and a room with a narrow bed and a sink. "You've made so many mistakes," whispered Correk.

He found Harkin in a backroom leaning over a replica of his old machine, carefully adjusting a bolt on the side. Harkin tweaked the wrench, giving a barely noticeable turn and stepped back. "I wasn't sure you would come." Harkin rubbed his sweaty palms on his tunic and smiled, doing his best to hide his nerves.

"Was that Peyton's room? It looks like a jail cell."

"It wasn't meant to be. It took a lot of energy to contain his fragmented magic. Anything bigger just didn't work." Harkin's voice was strained. "I should have asked for help."

"How did the Gardener talk you into taking him up on all of this?" Correk held out his arms.

Harkin let out a tired chuckle. "He doesn't exactly ask

questions and I was low on options." There was a long awkward pause until Harkin cleared his throat. "Do you want to see what I'm working on? It's a duplicate of the old machine..." He licked his dry lips.

"It's okay, I get it. The same kind of machine that harmed Peyton and got you sent to Trevilsom. Wasn't part of the sentence that you never try to build one of these again?"

Harkin tapped the palm of his hand with a wrench. "Yes, it was. But I couldn't leave Peyton the way he... he is. That's my doing. Ironic that having this machine may help stop Wolfstan."

"What do you mean?"

A smile played across Harkin's face and he turned, looking back to see if Correk would follow. "Wolfstan is trying to modify living organisms..."

"Animals, people, magicals."

"Well... uh, yes. He wants to modify them to give them enhanced abilities. From what I've seen of his work..." Harkin waved his hand, shaking his head. "Gruesome stuff. But from what I've seen it looks like he's trying to make them invulnerable to death. Replace the vital organs with magical artifacts and modern technology. Then, if an animal or a magical is shot in the torso..."

Correk took on a scowl. "The parts can be swapped out and they can continue. Is he building an army?"

"Most likely. I've heard rumors that he's selling shares in his company to wealthy humans who want to live forever. Greed is certainly a part of his calculations."

"But which world is he looking to monopolize?"

"Oh Earth, that much is obvious. Taking on Oricerans

directly would certainly lead to chaos. Not even the Dark Market would support him. He'd bring dark forces, rogues and kingdoms together to fight against him as one. But the humans are a different sort. Look at how they squabble already over finding artifacts."

Correk rubbed his chin. "By the time they caught on that it was in their best interests to unite, it would be too late."

"Exactly. But having the technology first gives us the opportunity to find a counter to it. You have to understand how something works in order to defeat it."

"That's impossible. We can't give back body parts that were taken. Stolen."

"That's where you may be wrong. It was in essence what I was trying to do for Peyton when he was dying. Regenerate a wounded body. But it went horribly wrong when his magic entered the machine and altered the settings. Technically it worked, just not the way it was intended. Come here, I'll show you." He walked with a lighter step, striding over to the large, gleaming white machine with a bed centered in the middle.

Correk's brow furrowed but he followed his father, walking all the way around the machine. "How do you test it without harming someone or something else?"

"That is a problem. The Gardener won't offer up an animal and it wouldn't answer the question of a magical being."

Correk crossed his arms over his chest and stood back, eyeing his father. "Was Peyton going to be your guinea pig, again?"

"No! No, never again." Harkin vigorously shook his

head. "I was wrong to do that. I'm not taking that back. I haven't answered that question yet. That's a large part of the delay."

"If Wolfstan got this far he would test it over and over again."

"I fear he is already doing that with his poorer rendition. He is a very clever, very dangerous and powerful foe. Never underestimate him. Many have and to their downfall. He understands dark magic, not as well as Rhazdon, but mixed with his knowledge of technology it makes him more dangerous. He needs to be dealt with in a permanent way. A half measure will only make things worse."

"We have a plan in motion."

"We... You mean the Jasper Elf, Leira Berens." Harkin tried to smile. "You have made a connection. A lasting one it appears."

"She is important to me."

"That is obvious. And she's bonded with a troll. You would have a troll in your life forever."

Correk arched an eyebrow and pursed his lips. "He grows on you... eventually."

"She reminds me of your mother. Spirited and knows her own mind."

"I didn't come here to talk about my mother..."

A trumpet blast split the air and Harkin reacted with blinding speed, his eyes taking on a glow and symbols appearing along his arms.

"What's happening?" Correk swung his bow around, already reaching for an arrow.

"It's the Gardener's alarm. Something has gone wrong." Harkin removed a piece from the machine and slipped it into his pocket. "That will disable it enough to lead anyone astray."

"You mean Wolfstan. You're worried he's found you." Correk pushed his way out the door to the small clearing by the building. His ears twitched, listening for the noise that was out of place.

The Gardener broke through the trees riding the large lion as Harkin came outside. "There's been a murder at the castle." The Gardener jumped off the lion's back as the lion let out a loud roar, turning his head to the side and shaking his mane. "An old Light Elf, Fraekin had his throat cut. Barbaric."

"Why is that a reason to sound the alarm back here?" Correk kept turning his head by degrees, still listening.

"The queen relived the event and saw the killer used shadow magic. No one could see him."

"Wolfstan," hissed Harkin.

"And at the last moment, he called out, *Harkin lives.* Your secret is out, and the queen is looking for you."

"She'll throw me in prison and ask questions later."

"Most likely. She hasn't completely forgiven you for what happened to Peyton. One of her favorites."

"He was wounded protecting her," said Correk. "She's extremely loyal. I had already proven myself at court. It was the only reason she let me stay." Correk waved his hand. "It's all in the past and should stay there. You need to leave. I'll take you back to Earth, beyond her jurisdiction."

"I'll hide him in the sanctuary near you," said the Gardener. "That will be safer. You need to get out of here too. You won't want to have to lie to Queen Saria."

"No, the queen would never forget a lie," said Harkin.

"Go back to Austin. I'll be okay and we can talk more about Wolfstan Humphrey later. Learn from my mistakes and let me help you." He looked around at the home he had known for years. "At least he hasn't found this place."

"We'll have to move the machinery too," said the Gardener. "Everything will be safer in the Texas sanctuary. I'm afraid your time here has come to an end, at least for a while."

Correk strapped his bow on his back and formed a ball of light in his hands, singing into it and pulling it apart. "I'll find you as soon as I can, Harkin. Wolfstan Humphrey has gotten our message and answered it with murder. We're going to need all the help we can get."

The patio at Estelle's was festooned with white papier mache streamers tied from tree to tree and glass bowls of white magnolias with thick green, leathery leaves floating in them. White linen tablecloths were thrown over the glass top tables near the corn hole pit and the side of the bar was draped with strings of little white lights along the front. The bigger picnic tables were moved to one side to leave room for dancing on the slate patio.

A *Closed for a Celebration* sign was hung on the front door, decorated with white roses.

Eireka and Don were under strict orders not to arrive early for the bridal shower that Cassidy and Kimberly kept calling the bride *and groom* shower. Mitzi rolled her eyes at that one but for once didn't add in her two cents. Leira, Correk and Mara were keeping them busy walking on

Main Street in nearby Fredericksburg, Texas. Yumfuck was neatly tucked in Leira's purse, lounging in a soft pair of panties, being kept quiet with samples from the different shops.

The regulars were back at Estelle's pitching in without being asked and were throwing orders back and forth at each other.

"Put the little fork on the outside. No, on top of the napkins."

"For Pete's sake, Craig, you're standing across from me. It's not a mirror. To your left. Other left."

"Okay, I got more ice. Where do I put it?"

"Hey, did anyone get those little colored mints? You know, the little pink and yellow ones. I love those."

"Mitzi, you're gonna have to hold Lemon. She's already licked the icing clean off one cupcake."

"Mike, did you bring the song list like I asked?"

"Oooh, we don't have much time left, we better get a move on."

Estelle came through the middle of the whirlwind, her red bouffant decorated with a small gold pixie hair clip, a cigarette dangling from her lips. She took a look at the progress and gave a satisfied nod to her head and went back to tend the smoker. She had been up since before the sunrise tending to the brisket and making sure the coolers were stocked with enough beer and there was enough whiskey behind the bar for everyone. Just this once, Estelle was going to break one of her own hard and fast rules and have an open bar.

She went and got on her stool and took the short stub of a cigarette out of her mouth, blowing out a perfect O, expertly blowing another, smaller O straight through the center. She chuckled and looked out over the patio, satisfied with the efforts. "Nothing but the best for the Berens' women," she said as she ground out the cigarette and headed inside.

"It's time! It's time!" Micky clapped her hands as Scott helped Mitzi check the tables one last time.

Toni, and some of the others from the Jackalope came in greeting the regulars like old friends. Kimberly and Paul made sure everyone had a cold drink in their hands as the volume quickly picked up. Eireka and Don came through the side gate unnoticed with Leira, Correk and Mara right behind them. They stood off to the side smiling and holding hands and waited for others to notice they had arrived.

Leira quietly slipped over to the guest house and went inside, carrying her purse to the couch. Yumfuck was out of the purse before it even landed, scrambling to the top of the couch and leaping off again, excited from the sounds of the party outside.

"I hate to do it to you, but this is Mom's day and she's earned it and then some. *Nesturnium.* Don't look at me like that. I'll bring you plenty of food all night long. Won't even make you wait till the end. And look, I got you all the Superman movies and even a Green Lantern and the old Wonder Woman TV show. Get a little Linda Carter action. You can spin around and… no? You'll have a blast. Wait, one more thing."

She ran to the kitchen and got the large container of cheese puffs down from the shelf in the pantry and went back to find the troll already working the remote.

"This should tide you over for a while. They're all yours."

"Trolls are great at parties, you know." He stuck his tongue out at her but finished with a cackle.

"Proven fact, I know. You'd even make a helluva deejay but maybe we don't educate the regulars today about the coming magic. How about we save that for say, after the wedding?"

"Your energy is different," squeaked Yumfuck. "Something about you has changed. You can get to your feelings more easily. What's up, sister? What'd you do?"

"Great, a nosey troll. I miss the days when you would mostly cackle at me. Mind your business. You don't see me asking you where you've been on your walkabouts, even after you managed to get so many hits with that reporter's video on YouTube. Or decided to do recon at Fleeker on your own."

"That was useful intel."

Leira kept going, ticking off each one. "And I could have sworn I smelled bacon on you once. Then there was the time you reeked of old lady perfume. I'm not sure I even wanted to know…"

"Okay, okay. Point taken. Have a good time." He blew her a raspberry as he pulled out a cheese puff, smelling it first before opening his mouth wide and pushing it in, chomping as fast as he could till it was gone. "And repeat…"

"I'm out of here. Better there are no witnesses to what you're about to do with that entire jar." She glanced at the ceiling and the perfectly round orange circles. "I'll paint over those someday."

Leira straightened the front of her green dress and stepped outside, closing the door behind her. Eireka and Don were surrounded by people asking them questions, admiring the ring and making toasts. Correk was standing back with a beer in his hand, smiling. Leira went and stood next to him, taking his beer from his hand and taking a long swig, handing it back.

"You look pretty good in a suit. You should try it more often."

"I've needed more battle gear during my time on Earth than suits. Maybe something flame retardant. Too soon? You look pretty good in a dress. Reminds me of that ball we went to in Chicago."

"Seems like a million years ago, now. So much has happened."

Correk put his hand in the small of Leira's back and rested it there as Estelle passed behind them, a new cigarette dangling from her lips. "Bout dang time," she said, without breaking her stride. "Here, you can have your own beer and swap spit later." She handed Leira a Shiner Bock and took Correk's empty bottle from his hand, handing him another.

Leira looked at the smile across her mother's face and at Toni and Mara laughing, their mouths wide open and heads back. "I want to remember this moment forever. It's perfect. I have everything I want and then some."

Correk saw the flash of pain come across her face. "It will last, and if it doesn't, we will rebuild it together."

"I know that darkness is coming and harder times. I can feel it and all the signs are flashing it like neon on a no-tell motel." She shook her head, determined. "Nope, today we celebrate this. Just this. A little piece of happiness between two people who waited a helluva of a long time to be together."

"I went to see Harkin in his lab."

"Bold move. Did you get the answers you needed?"

"Some... enough for now."

The gate opened and Hagan stood there in his best suit, holding it open for Rose who was carrying a pie.

"Felix, you came!" Eireka broke away from the cluster of people around her and went to greet them.

"I made a pie, I hope you don't mind," said Rose. "I know the invitation said no gifts, but I wanted to bring a little something from us. Oh, the tables look lovely! Felix and I are so happy for you."

Leira came and stood beside Hagan, giving him a dead fish look.

"What's the look for, Berens?"

"Just getting used to everyone calling you, Felix. It's an adjustment."

"It's my great-grandfather's name, a distinguished cowboy in his days from these parts. This is a great day, Berens. Even left my gun at home in the lock box. Rose insisted, but I would have done it anyway. Boy, when I first met you, I did not see the story taking a turn like this. I mean, you were holding it together just fine, but I saw you more as a great cop and a permanent loner. Now, you're a great Fed and surrounded by people." He shook his head with a chuckle "You might just make an optimist out of me yet. Well, if it weren't for all the dark magic running loose."

"Yeah, there's still that... but today there's this. Our family grows by one more and he's a good one."

Rose was moving through the crowd occasionally looking back at Hagan and Leira.

"How's Rose adjusting to knowing magic is real?"

"Better than I thought she would. Of course, I left out all the dark and harrowing parts, but I did that when I was working homicide. It's bad enough we have to know the darker side of all kinds of beings. You know, I don't think you're supposed to be hanging back here with me. Go greet your guests, be with your mother and grandmother and make some good memories. Store them up..."

"...in the face of what's to come."

Hagan hesitated but finally shrugged. "Well, yeah... maybe. Or maybe it will just be for your old age. Go, I'm gonna get a beer and chat up a few of the regulars about bowling. Maybe even join the team."

Hagan turned to go toward the bar just as Estelle walked by him holding out a cold Rocket 100 still in the can. She didn't even break stride. "God, I love that woman," he said, taking a deep swig.

Leira was already getting a tight hug from Toni, her soft afro bobbing with her excitement. Hagan let out a troubled sigh, making sure to keep a smile on his face as he made his way around to Correk. Michael held up his beer in a toast as the gathering all cheered and Hagan held up his as he sidled up next to Correk.

"I was listening to the police scanner on the way over here. Habit. There was interesting chatter about something weird going down at the Driskill Hotel. Something about a hairy beast changing into a man and leaving a big mess on the third floor. A lot of unidentified goo left everywhere."

Correk's eyes grew wide and he turned to look at Hagan, his eyes narrowing.

"No, no," said Hagan, "this is a party. Nothing we can do about it now. Keep a smile planted on your face for those three women over there. If you don't, I'm pretty sure the tiny redheaded one who runs this show will do a fine job of kicking your ass."

Hagan forced himself to relax and take in slow, even breaths. "The world in between is even spitting out shifters."

"Shifters with a dark cloud kind of trailing behind them. Maybe the thing has finally taken shape."

"When this party is over, we will go check it out."

Neither one noticed Turner Underwood standing behind them, a pink rose in his lapel, leaning forward, resting on his cane. "I have a better idea, gentlemen."

"You really have to teach me how you do that one, Turner." Correk took a sip of his beer to hide being startled all over again by the old Fixer.

"It's in those books. Takes years of practice to get it just right. Fun at parties, too." He smiled but his eyes were icy. "Correk, find me later. I have an old friend I want to introduce you to. For now, how about we drop the shop talk and enjoy the day. I hear there's brisket!"

Correk waded back into the center of the party as the toasts progressed until Estelle made everyone get in line and eat till they couldn't move. Craig threatened to undo the top button of his pants but one look from Mitzi and he dropped the idea. Even Lemon got her fill of brisket and true to her word, Leira dropped off food with the troll. Enough to keep him happy.

The sun was setting by the time the last stragglers finally, happily left through the bar, slapping each other on the back and laughing together. Only Hagan and Rose, Turner Underwood and Leira and Correk were left. Even the happy couple had headed off together somewhere and Estelle was busy in the kitchen directing the staff in the cleanup.

"I'm going to drop Rose off, and I'll meet you fellas down on 6th Street."

"No need, dear. I'll take the car. You can ride with them." Rose gave him a patient smile and picked up the empty pie plate. "You go to work. I'll see you at home." She kissed him on the cheek as Estelle rushed out of the restaurant with a bag of leftovers for her. "Thank you, Estelle! I'll make sure Felix parcels these out over a few days."

"Instead of a few hours…" whispered Leira.

"I heard that." Hagan pressed his lips together.

"I meant for you to."

"See those two already have their heads together. I've seen that before. Start of another adventure. I'll see myself out the side gate. Get to it, dear!"

"Yes honey." Hagan waved to Rose as Estelle gave a satisfied nod, blowing out smoke that encircled her head momentarily in a grey cloud. She marched back into the bar and headed for the kitchen, throwing a bar towel over her shoulder.

"Okay, spill it. You guys have been more than your usual amount of weird all day. I appreciate that you did your best to hide it but the party's over. What's happened?" Leira crossed her arms over her chest and cocked her hip, waiting.

"Where to begin…" Turner tapped his cane on the ground. Leira knew by now that meant he was buying time trying to figure out how to ease into something. *This is bad.*

"Okay, Hagan, you start. What do you know? I checked my phone. There's no messages from the general."

"Something slimy creeped its way out of the world in between from our favorite room at the Driskill Hotel and allegedly pulled off a werewolf kind of transformation."

"A fucking shifter from the world in between," Leira said in a hush. "No…"

"Thank you, Hagan. That's the best segue I've ever been given. Leads nicely to my piece of this story." Turner placed a heavy hand on Correk's tall shoulder, holding him firmly. "That beast was once known as Lucius about eight hundred years ago."

Correk's entire body shook as he did his best to absorb the information. "No… not possible." He flexed the muscles in his legs, determined to stay standing.

"Lucius fought bravely in the wars against Rhazdon and was believed dead even though we never found a body. There were some who believed Rhazdon did something to him but none of us ever imagined the bitch went this far."

"What do you mean, this far? What does all this mean?" Leira played with the bracelet on her wrist.

"She threw a spell on him just before she tore an opening in the veil and threw him in. Rhazdon knows how to make shifters without all the need for experimentation."

Correk balled his hands into fists, breathing hard. "Lucius was protecting the old king. Rhazdon must have thrown both of them into the world in between."

"I think the king falling into the void was a happy accident for Rhazdon. It was Lucius she was cursing to hell and back. The back from hell part has finally shown up and he's out there on the loose."

"Searching for Rhazdon. That's a wide swath of destruction to try and dig her out of whatever hole she climbed into. It could be anywhere on two different worlds." Leira looked toward the guest house where the troll was ensconced. "Things are getting more complicated."

"Lucius isn't himself and we don't know what the curse and hundreds of years in that isolation void of slime has done to his mind." Turner tapped his cane hard against the ground. "His lust for revenge of some kind makes him unstable."

"Not to mention the whole fur and fang thing. Okay, we are forewarned." Leira held up her hand before Correk or Hagan could say it. "And I'll keep the troll close. I'm not going to pretend I can handle all of this. Things have taken a turn for the hairy weird."

"And around here that's saying something. I suppose we should consider ourselves fortunate that Wolfstan Humphrey has been so quiet. For now..." Turner let out a weary laugh. "Alright, time to get moving. Correk, I have an assignment for you, if you can break away. Nothing important you were doing?"

Correk made a point of not looking up at Leira who was giving him a crooked smile. "I'm all yours. Ready to be of service."

"Go get 'em!" Leira patted him hard on the back as Hagan narrowed his eyes, watching the two of them.

"Uh huh," he muttered. "I see..."

CHAPTER ELEVEN

"**D**id you get some kind of signal?" Correk was looking around for signs of trouble standing out on Rainey Street but things were quiet. Tourists walked up and down, mixing with the college students who were always near the food trucks or going in and out of the bars.

Turner Underwood smiled wearily and cocked his head to the side. "I am actually not sure what to do next. It's been years since that has happened to me and not a good look on a Fixer." He placed his hand on Correk's shoulder, one hand still on his cane.

Correk looked at the hand, skeptical. "The last time you did that you told me Lucius is a cursed beast back from the ancient past. Is this your tell?"

"Do you trust me?"

"With my life."

"Good answer. Spoken like a worthy Light Elf and new Fixer."

"You're not taking down your hand."

The Fixer thought about it and slowly removed his

hand. "This one is going to have to be a show and tell deal. Come on, there's a mission at hand but first we need to make a stop at my house."

Turner Underwood drove his early model Bentley up the curved driveway with Correk sitting in the passenger seat. He had owned the sleek black Mark IV since it was brand new in 1946 and they had both aged well together. He dreaded what he was about to do as much as he was filled with joy for both of them. Things were changing rapidly, and the old rules were breaking down. The return of the old King was a welcome reprieve but the veil that kept in the world in between was breaking down.

Who knows what else is lurking in there?

"You haven't said a word the entire drive." Correk glanced over at Turner as he opened the door and stepped out of the car.

"Words fail for some things. Come with me."

The old Fixer waved his hand as he approached the large wooden front door, pin curls of light shooting out and unlocking the door, swinging it wide. He moved quickly through the house to the far wing, not looking back at Correk as he went. He got to the sitting room where he usually put guests and gave a soft tap as he opened the door.

The old King of Oriceran sat in an upholstered blue linen chair by the window looking out over the lake. "It's the simple things you miss the most. You wouldn't think it would be sitting in a chair quietly watching a heron land on a lake but it's the sweetest thing I've seen in far too many years."

Correk let out an audible gasp and crossed the room swiftly, kneeling on one knee in front of the old King.

"Your Majesty... How? After the battle I thought you were wounded."

The king looked up, a cold look in his eyes. "Wounded takes on different meanings in the world in between. There's time to heal most things or for things to fester." He got up out of the chair as Correk stood and he hugged him tightly, slapping his back. "I knew your grandfather. Good Light Elf. You look just like him!" He stood back and saw the pain in Correk's face. "I hear your father has made an appearance. Turner has been catching me up. You were fairly young when he disappeared. Someday I will have to tell you stories of your grandfather. I may help you see your father in a different light. For now, apparently, there's no time to let things unfold."

"Too many beasts running loose of every ilk," said Turner, as he swept his arm around the room, setting loose more pinwheels of light. "You can never be too careful. A little added protection these days will go a long way. Have you finished the third tome of spells?"

"I'm onto the fifth book... making progress." Correk kept studying the king's face.

"Good... then you are ready for your first solo mission. I need you to head out to San Francisco to rescue a teenager. Correk, are you paying attention?"

"I'm real, not an hallucination," said the old king. "Tell me how you are doing. You must be well over a hundred years now. Have you taken a wife yet?"

Turner let out a cough, changing the subject. "We will table that discussion for another day. Correk you are needed elsewhere." The Fixer pulled the light between his hands, forming a ball and singing into it, stretching it out to make a portal. "San Francisco awaits you. Everything you need is on this paper," he said, handing him a folded note. "We like to keep things simple. Get to the youngest son of the family at this address. He's a clever young Wizard who's been fiddling with dark magic and playing a local gang off against some rival Wizards. No one is happy with him, including the Silver Griffins. Take him to the second address. A school is starting there on an old piece of property I own outside of Charlottesville, Virginia. I made a deal with your General Anderson." Turner shook his head. "Go… part of being the Fixer is thinking on your feet. You'll figure out the rest."

Correk nodded to the old king. "We will talk more when I return."

"I look forward to it." The king smiled at Correk, even as he gripped the sides of the chair.

Correk stepped through the portal, looking back as it closed behind him. The king looked at Turner. "Someone will need to tell my son that I have returned."

"Not yet. Not till we find Lucius."

"And figure out what to do with him."

"Indeed…" Turner felt the weight of a thousand years and settled heavily into a chair, drawing himself up, his cane settled against a wall. He held up his hand. "Patience. Let me work in peace." The old spell came easily to his lips as he ran through it quickly, pronouncing every syllable in rapid succession, He shut his eyes as the acrid smell of sulphur filled his nostrils, burning the inside of his nose. "Lucius still remembers some of his past. He's cloaking himself well... but not perfectly." Turner opened his eyes and got to his feet. "I'm off. You have the run of the house."

"Not so fast. I'm coming with you. Lucius is my friend. He gave his life to protect me so I'm partially responsible for what he's become. This isn't a discussion."

"Doesn't take long to get back into the monarch groove, does it?" He gave the king a wry smile. "If you're coming, get your ass up and move it, your majesty." He gave a slight nod in deference.

The king easily rose to his feet. "Times really have changed."

"Yes, you are still a strapping, powerful Light Elf and I'm a cantankerous powerful old Light Elf. That makes me the more dangerous of the two of us."

"Time doesn't move in the void. A curse for the most part. Let's get on with it. Lucius was a powerful warrior in his day, and he's had hundreds of years to plot his revenge."

CHAPTER TWELVE

L eira opened the door to the guest house and found the troll sleeping in the potted fern near the couch, his belly full. "Hate to wake you, little dude but we have business to get to." She nudged him, watching him uncurl, stretching out his tiny legs and letting out a wide yawn. He opened his eyes and looked up at Leira, letting out a cackle followed quickly by a gassy burp. Leira stood up straight, batting at the air in front of her. "Oh gawd, fuck, what is that? What did you eat while I was gone? Part of the sofa?"

The troll let out another cackle and stood up in the dirt, rubbing his back against the smooth green leaves. "What you want? We have a mission?"

"Don't know if I'd say we're going on a mission. Little dramatic Elwood. More like a look and see for shifters."

The troll bounded out of the plant and hopped to the couch, his claws digging in as he pulled himself up to the top. "Ooooh, that's some bad shit." He tied his cape around his shoulders and pulled on the mask.

"Is that really necessary? Do you need to hide your

identity?"

"Meh, it's a look. Where we headed?"

"That's the tricky part. Hop on while I see if I can use myself like a magical GPS and get a better idea of location." Leira held out her hand as the troll climbed into her palm and she lifted him to her shoulder. She shut her eyes and pulled in energy through her feet, feeling it surge through her as she set out an intention. *Find the shifter. Show me his location.*

The stream of magic doubled over on itself, knocking Leira forward as she let out a soft grunt and Yumfuck held on to her jacket, his fur bristling from the energy passing under his feet.

Leira felt a burning sensation in the scar on her belly as the energy lifted her onto her toes. *The stronger the intention, the more powerful the surge of magic.* Turner Underwood's words echoed in her head.

"Find the shifter," she whispered. She felt the magic pull her out onto the light stream as images flashed on either side of her. She breathed in suddenly... *a sweet aroma... grapes. No, wait, this is different.*

She passed over acres of grapes growing on wooden trellises to a large white stucco house with a clay tile roof in the distance. The closer they got, the more Leira could feel the presence of dark energy moving around the house. The energy slipped in easily and she found herself rolling along a long, cool hallway lined with empty oak wooden barrels on either side. *Don't argue with the energy. It knows what it's doing.* More of Turner's wisdom, keeping Leira from short-circuiting her request. *This is not where he was being held.*

The energy hesitated, feeling her distrust as she made herself take a deep breath and let it out.

"Relax!" shouted the troll into her ear. She heard it like a squeaky echo through the thick ribbons of magic surrounding her.

Leira felt the magic slowing as it curled up to a thick metal door, easily passing through like vapor. On the other side of the door was an old storage room, dank and dark with a high ceiling.

Leira could hear grunting and something scraping along the cement floor. She drew back in the living room of the guest house, a shudder passing through her. *There must be close to a hundred.* A shifter screamed out in anger. They were packed in like cattle, some clawing each other in frustration or boredom, shifting in and out of human and beast. The energy rolled around the room, hugging the wall till it got to a back corner and stopped, hovering near the ceiling.

Standing with his back against the wall was the man Leira had seen before. She took in every detail of his description, memorizing his face. She felt a shift in the energy as he jerked his face up and looked directly at her. *That's fucking impossible!*

Leira saw the anger in his eyes, an absence of fear, unlike the others who were an even mixture of both. *Who are you?*

"Find the location!" Yumfuck was yelling in her ear again. "Keep your eye on the ball," he squeaked. "Tell the motherfucking energy what you want!"

Show me the location.

The energy pulled out of the room as Leira kept

looking back at the man standing naked in the large room till she couldn't see him anymore over the sea of bodies. Leira felt the energy pass through the wall and found herself back outside, moving around a large estate. *Show me where I am.* Her frustration grew as the magic went in circles, creating whirls of light.

"Focus!" chirped the troll as he pinched the skin along her neck.

Leira instinctively raised a hand to slap at the bite but Yumfuck jumped out of the way, cackling. "Son of a bitch! Like being bit by a greenheaded mosquito!"

Okay, focus. The energy knows what it's doing. What are we circling? In and out and around the magic went, as Leira saw the name. Icardi. It was on everything. Stamped on barrels, hanging on a sign above the door of the building, on labels of bottles of wine. The Icardi vineyards, established 1989, Napa, California. It was a staging ground. *Got it.*

Leira felt the rush of energy pull through her, running like a river. It was familiar but still uncomfortable as the magic drained quickly out of her, snapping her back into her body. Her mouth popped open, sucking in air as she opened her eyes. The troll was leaning out from her shoulder staring at her, inches from her face. "Ready to go?"

"What the fuck? That's disturbing. Personal space, Yumfuck. Yeah, ready to go. Need one more thing before we go. I don't think this one is gonna be pretty and I'm keeping my word. No running into the burning buildings by myself anymore."

CHAPTER THIRTEEN

L eira stood on the edge of the vineyards near the road. Yumfuck stood on her shoulder wearing his cape and mask. "You know that cape and mask won't work when you grow into battle size."

"Works for now. I'll keep it on a little longer. Trouble ahead." The troll glanced backward. "Little trouble back there too."

Behind them an open portal crackled and sparked.

Leira rolled her eyes and picked up a pebble from the ground throwing it into the portal. "Hurry your ass up before it closes. I thought you used these things all the time."

"That's how you tear a hole in the veil." Louie poked his head out of the opening and stepped out, stamping his feet on the dirt path as the portal finally closed. The sword was strapped to his back. "Used portals all the time in my previous profession." He brushed off his suede pants and looked around at the vines and up at the open sky.

MARTHA CARR & MICHAEL ANDERLE

"Stealing." Leira recognized the way the vines were laid out and could see the tops of buildings in the distance.

"Acquiring. Not a bad place for a hunt."

"Not sure if we're here for a hunt or a rescue, or both."

"Oh, this is a hunt, trust me. Only question of the day will be if we're the ones being hunted, and that answer may vary hour to hour. The dark Wizarding families don't play well with others and have only one rule. Beat the shit out of their opponents. That would be us today."

Leira flexed her hands and circled her arms. "Wouldn't mind doing a little shit kicking myself today. Been awhile."

"You have a plan about how we go in there?" Louie pulled the sword out of its sheath on his back and held it up in front, limbering up for the fight. "Or do we wander through the grapevines and start the party early."

"We go in under a glamour that won't hold the closer we get. And then we take down as many as we can. Our goal is to let out the shifters."

Louie stopped moving the sword back and forth and wrinkled his forehead. "What the fuck are you talking about, lady? Isn't that the army we will have to fight?"

"I'm guessing that's not the whole truth."

"Fuckin' A. And you're guessing our limbs at best and our lives at worst if you're wrong."

"Something like that." Leira was making herself take measured breaths, feeling the energy trails around her. Traces of dark energy were everywhere but all of them fading. "The families are out… or at least most of them are. We might just have the element of surprise. I don't think they realized we could find them so easily."

"Then let's get to it. Find out if a shifter still has a conscience... or even thinks at all because we roll like that."

Leira pulled in energy through her feet, letting it power up through her spine and out her hands, the symbols appearing, flashing over and over as her eyes glowed. The air shimmered around them as they became transparent to anyone looking out of a window, invisibly moving through the vineyard.

Louie glanced over at Leira's arms trying to read some of the symbols, his eyes widening as he saw the rapid report. "For the love of... your magic is predicting outcomes. Fuck... we do not win in all of them."

"What's the fun in knowing you will win? Odds never been against you before?"

"That's kind of an average day for me." Louie let out a sigh and gripped the sword tighter. *Stay aware.* The sword was speaking to him again. He was taking small comfort from the lack of general panic from the weapon.

"You look a little freaked out, Louie. Jackson led me to believe you'd seen your fair share of shit going down."

"That's usually shit I'm actively running from with some sweet prize in my possession. I'm a virgin at seeking it out and walking right into it." They were midway through the vineyards as Louie saw something pass an upstairs window of one of the buildings. He instinctively stopped and had to walk faster to catch up with Leira. She had made peace with what was to come, and her jaw was set. "Damn, girl, I take it going at trouble is kind of your thing."

"You might say that. More of a career for me. Okay,

from here out we go silent. You watch me for signals. No one should be able to see us…"

"Should?"

"There's very powerful old magic used here. The kind that's supposed to be illegal on both planets. I can't guarantee we won't step over some line and find ourselves bare naked so to speak."

"Great. And we're an army of two… You never did answer me. Before we go in, how many shifters are we setting loose?"

"It's an army of three. Don't count out Yumfuck. He'll rip off a few heads if necessary. I'd say about a hundred or so beasts, give or take."

"A hundred…"

"Okay, silence…"

Louie mouthed *motherfuckers*, as he gripped the sword even tighter. Leira didn't even flinch as she approached the warehouse.

CHAPTER FOURTEEN

Leira and Louie got to the other side of the vineyards. A large gravel opening separated them from a main house to the left and a large warehouse directly in front that stretched to the right. Large aluminum roll doors were standing open just to the right.

"Security seems a little lax." Louie peered into the darkness of the warehouse, noting a door at the far side and another opening at the back.

Yumfuck ran down Leira's arm and dropped to the ground. His fur was standing on end. He took off at a run and smelled around the door deep inside the warehouse, instantly growing to his full height at eight feet, standing back, waiting for Leira's command. "Smells like dogs. A lot of them."

Leira could feel it too. "Or shifters. That's not all. They left a few assholes to watch the place," she whispered. "They know we're here." Leira could see the rolls of glittering dark magic billowing out from the building, signaling someone's approach. *Too late to get more help.*

"Then we fight," whispered Louie.

"If it's the last good thing we do."

"With honor and to the end."

"Come on, motherfuckers," growled the troll. Louie looked up at the troll in surprise just as Emerick appeared in the large opening of the warehouse, a sneer on his face.

"Hate it when the assholes like to make grand entrances." Leira stuck to Hagan's rules. *Let the idiots go first.* Several of his cousins appeared behind him, Toby off to the far left, sweating profusely, his eyes wide.

The troll opened his mouth wide, letting out a roar that rumbled along the ground hitting them in a sound wave that knocked over a smaller witch near the front. She scrambled back to her feet, her face beet red with embarrassment and anger.

Hold the sword out in front and point the tip toward them. Louie knew enough to just follow the sword's lead. His muscles rippled along his arms as he waited, tense.

The symbols along Leira's arms and neck glowed as the glamour peeled away from them, revealing where they stood. The symbols flashed, turning over like a fast-moving ticker. Toby trembled where he stood but he didn't dare run. Emerick would have cut him down before he got very far.

"Leira Berens," Emerick taunted. "Thanks for making this convenient."

"I hate pissants. This would be annoying Hagan if he were here."

"Funny you should mention him." Lois emerged out of the vineyards to Leira's right. "Don't be mad. I had Hagan put a tracker on your skin. I knew you'd think bringing one Wizard and a swearing troll would count as asking for help. Besides, it was a slow day. Hagan's acting as backup back at the ranch." Lois held out her wand. "Hello Emerick. Haven't seen you since your christening. Cried the entire time."

Emerick frowned, looking around nervously. "Hello Aunt Lois. This isn't your fight."

Leira looked back and forth between the two. "Don't know when you got here, Lois but I'm glad to see you. You sure you can fight family?"

"This is awkward," said Louie.

"Not my first time, sadly. This is the dark branch of the family. We're all overachievers, it's just some of us had different ambitions." Lois raised her wand and pointed it at Emerick, scowling. "Raise your hand to a friend of mine, Emerick and you make it my fight. Back up now and we'll walk away."

"No, we won't. I came here for a reason. Not leaving till it's done." Leira took a step forward as she formed a fireball between her hands. Set an intention. She pitched it right at Emerick's chest and watched as he raised his wand, frantically whispering a spell. Lois watched in horror, not sure what to do as the fireball split apart at the last moment hitting the front line of millennial witches and wizard, spraying fiery buckshot, setting small blazes on their clothes. A few dropped their wands, busy patting down their shirts or the crotch of their pants.

Emerick regained his composure first, countering with a spell to douse the flames. The thin smile returned to his lips as he glanced behind him. He retreated back, enticing Leira to follow him.

"About time," she growled. She formed another fireball and aimed it at Emerick's feet, knocking him down. The game was growing tiring.

"So far this is too fucking easy." Louie followed close behind her as Lois took up the rear, easily countering the spells of the young wizards and witches. Toby hung back in the shadows, watching. He had always liked Aunt Lois. He never expected to have to fight her. Besides, the stories about her were legendary.

Leira crept forward, entering the large building into the main area used for tastings and large parties. Small tables standing at chest height were dotted around the room and a long bar was across the back. To the right was the door Leira was looking for that led to the old storage partially underground.

A padlock on the door. Seems old school.

Sirius appeared out of the shadows and waved his wand knocking the wind out of Leira sending her into the air, rolling like a barrel before dropping her hard to the ground. Instincts took over and she rolled to her feet, crouched low. The troll growled in anger and took a long swipe at Emerick, nicking the skin along his face and drawing a thin line of blood. Emerick raised his wand as the troll swiped again, snapping the maple wood easily in two, leaving a gash across Emerick's hand.

Lois raised her wand and sent Emerick flying, slamming him into a far wall and knocking him out. "For his own good."

Louie rushed forward, the sword directing him to swing wide as the tip cut a gash in a witch's arm causing her to cry out and drop her wand. Leira saw Sirius smile and Leira realized they were being baited with the younger set, drawn further into the building.

That's okay, motherfuckers. I see it coming.

Leira heard the howling and grunting as the ground thundered beneath them. Sirius suddenly turned and pointed his wand at the padlock, easily unlocking it with a simple spell. The door burst open, pushing off its hinges as the shifters finally got their first full taste of freedom, starved for days. They were hungry for any kind of meat they could find and weren't in a picky mood.

"Shit just got very deep in here." Louie swung his sword at the beasts as it sang out a metallic note in the air. Leira volleyed fireballs, breaking apart into small pea-sized scattershot, keeping them at bay, but just barely. She kept an eye on Sirius off to the side who was hungrily watching his experiment, hoping for a bloody success story.

"You're still just as annoying as ever, brother." Lois waved her wand in a circle over her head and sent out a lasso of light encircling Sirius, binding his arms to his side. He easily broke through it, a guttural laugh escaping his lips as he held onto one end of the lasso, snapping it back at Lois, whipping her across the chest.

"You've always underestimated me, sister. By the way, it was me who broke your favorite figurine when you were ten."

"Fuck me, they're having a reunion," yelled Louie as he raised the sword over his head, ready to make his first kill of the night. "One beastie down, 99 left to go. Might make a nifty drinking song."

"No!" yelled Leira, as she eyed the bracelet on her wrist. *Last measures, it comes off.* She scanned the group, looking for the man she had seen earlier but there was no human among them. They were all transformed into beasts. This may not work. The horde of claws and fangs approached, slashing the air in front of them.

"Leira, you're gonna have to get over this and let me take out a few or we're dinner. There's not much choice here."

Leira glanced over to make sure Lois was keeping Sirius busy as she sent out waves of energy shoving the beasts back just enough to buy time. "He's in here... I know it. Show yourself!" Her chest heaved up and down from breathing so hard to contain the energy it took to push them back inches, their claws waving just in front of her face. She wasn't going to be able to do it for much longer unless the bracelet came off. *I'm risking Louie and Yumfuck.* The troll sensed her reluctance to kill and stood by her side, towering over her, howling at the shifters.

Leira pushed the thread of energy into the mass of twisting bodies. *Trust the magic.*

A howl erupted from the center, loud and angry, echoing off the tin ceiling. The mass of fur fell back, still growling as they moved away from Leira, crouching down just enough for the beast who had let out the howl to do it again.

"Thank God, the alpha. I was right."

"You were gambling?"

"Louie, in case you haven't noticed the fucking world has changed and everything is pretty much a gamble from here on out. Get used to it." Leira kept her eyes on the silverback as he reared his head back and howled again. He lowered his chin and stared into Leira's eyes. A cold, hungry glare with his teeth bared.

"Just because we found the alpha doesn't mean he's up for bargaining."

"Attack!" Sirius sent out sparks from his wand, sending small currents of pain into the crowd of shifters.

Leira saw her chance and turned on Sirius directing everything at him and removing her energy from the pack of human wolves hungry to eat something. She wrapped Sirius as tightly as she could in waves of energy, squeezing tight as the air rushed out of his lungs.

The pack inched closer to her, glancing back toward the alpha. Leira's arms were straining as she pressed Sirius' ribs in on his heart. The muscles along her neck stood out against the symbols as Yumfuck moved to be right by her side.

Leira looked directly at the alpha and yelled, "Run! Run motherfuckers, run!"

The alpha growled and dropped to all fours running, right at Leira, as Louie raised his sword to defend her.

"No! We stand our ground."

Louie kept the sword raised, ready to strike if he had to, but the alpha veered at the last moment, brushing against Leira, running toward the path that led between the trellises, swiping at the tender vines as he went. Leira felt the wiry hair brush against her arm, close enough to feel the warmth and the coiled muscle. The pack all dropped to the ground, quickly following their new leader, streaming around Louie, Lois and Leira, brushing against them as they ran past. Yumfuck growled as they moved around him, staying close to Leira. A writhing, steady stream of beasts, some still emerging from the depths below.

"It's a fucking muscular fur blanket," Louie whispered in awe, as he held perfectly still, letting them pass. A sea of shifters that could tear them apart and stretched out as far as they could see till most of the beasts passed them by and ran into the dimming light of the day.

Leira still held on to Sirius, letting the magic pulse toward him as her lip curled. She felt the bile rise in her throat as she bore down on Sirius till she heard the inevitable crack of his ribs.

"Stop! You're not a killer. Not like this!" Lois yelled out but made no attempt to stop Leira. She was pretty sure she couldn't even if she wanted to. In all her years in the Silver Griffins, Lois had never seen a power surge like she was witnessing build in Leira.

Leira swallowed hard and let him drop to the ground, not moving. "He's still alive. That may prove to be a mistake. Louie, circle around the back of the house, make sure nothing else is coming."

Louie doubled back, keeping his eyes on the different Witches and Wizards until he was able to clear the far side of the wide opening, large enough to drive trucks in side by side. He ran as fast as he could around the back, leaping over a pile of carefully wound hoses, and crossing over a small courtyard.

Turn and swing the sword at an angle to the right holding your arm close to your body.

He did as he was told and swung hard, cutting off the tip of a Wizard's wand just as he was about to finish the spell that came out in a quickly fading mumble. Louie curled his lip and realized the sword had gotten him to hold back from wounding the Wizard. He thought about taking out just one of these dark pawns but the sounds of howling and barking from the distant vineyards and shouting from the other side of the building stopped him.

"Another time," he said, menacingly and pushed the tip into the ribs of the Wizard, nicking his shirt and easily tearing a gaping hole. The Wizard turned and ran, looking back over his shoulder as Louie got to the back of the main house and ran inside, quickly covering the first floor. He saw the back of Juliana standing at the front door but left her alone. "Best not poke that dog just yet."

He got to the large kitchen and opened every door, searching for hidden stairs or anyone hiding. Nothing. He ran down a long hall, away from the front door and stopped at the entrance to an office with bookshelves that went from floor to a vaulted ceiling, completely filled with books. "Mother lode," he whispered. He ran over and touched the spine of the closest shelf. "Just what I thought... ancient spell books. Fuck... what to take. What to take."

He took out his wand, whispering a spell, the sword still in his other hand, its voice a constant in the back-ground chatter in his head. *Run outside... now... run outside... now.* For once, he ignored it.

"Something like this is never coming around again." He shook his head, squeezing his eyes shut. *Run outside... now... run outside...now.* He raised his wand, even as he gripped the handle of the sword, whispering a finder's spell. He saw a book flutter on an upper shelf. "Gotcha."

Run outside... now... run outside...now. The sword became more urgent. "I will. Fuck! I will. One more minute." He ran to the library ladder and slid it across the track running along the top, jumping on as he pulled till it came to rest just under the shelf where the book was still vibrating.

Leira needs you. Run outside... now... run outside...now. The dark mist approaches. Choose.

Louie was halfway up the ladder. "Are you fucking kidding me?"

He looked up at the shelf just as he heard a crack of electricity coming from the front of the house and smelled a foul odor. He looked up at the book one last time, grabbing a random book, and leapt for the ground. "You are becoming someone I don't recognize, Louie. Uh huh, now we're talking to ourselves in the third person." He hesitated at the door to the library and spun his wand in a tight circle, creating a blue transparent fireball at the tip, lobbing it at the nearest shelves, igniting the old books instantly. The fire quickly spread as he whispered a spell to make sure it couldn't be easily extinguished.

"Man, that hurt. I'm actually picking sides." He ran for the nearest side door, running back to the open ground between the vineyards and the set of buildings, emerging in time to see someone run out of the house, ignorant of what he had just done.

CHAPTER FIFTEEN

"No!" A screech emerged from the nearby house as Agnes came running, throwing herself down by Sirius, checking his wounds. Juliana let her pass but stayed in the doorway.

Leira saw Louie run into the open. *She's too calm.* Leira assessed the Witch with the same calculations she had been using as Hagan's partner. *The bitch is up to something.* Her breathing stayed even. *No point in freaking out till I have to... if I have to. Another Hagan rule.*

Juliana had the smallest of smiles as she raised both arms, her wand extended. "Tenebris infinitum!"

Leira felt the hairs along her arms stand up straight and a cold chill go down her back. She recognized all the signs easily by now. The dark mist was approaching. *This was their plan all along.* "Takes the idea of shit storm to a whole new level."

"What?" Louie ran back to defend Leira from behind, putting himself back by the door to the storage as the last of the shifters finally lumbered up the stairs, looking around for a moment, teeth bared, growling. Only the intermittent howl of the newly established alpha got them to reluctantly keep moving. "There's always a few who don't fit in as well as the others. I ought to know..."

Leira felt the tug of the dark magic as the light energy responded in kind, springing to life inside of her, barely being held in check by the artifact on her arm.

The blue flames from the main house were reaching the roof line and smoke was billowing out of upstairs windows.

"The library!" Some of the Witches and Wizards ran toward the house but Juliana refused to move, her mouth twitching with anger. It was too late. She had made her choice.

Leira slowly turned, her jaw set as her muscles tensed and her eyes glowed in the growing darkness while she watched a black mist curl out across acres of vineyard. Sweat trickled down the side of her face. She put one hand across the bracelet, ready to rip it off but at the last moment whispered fervently, "Grandmother, join me."

Louie looked back over his shoulder in the direction of Leira's gaze and took a step back, nudging the last of the shifters running by, earning a deep scratch down his thigh for his troubles. He screamed out in pain and raised his sword, stopping himself at the last moment as the beast kept running, answering the howl of the alpha somewhere in the distance.

"Fuck! Son of a bitch! It's easier when I can kill something, ask questions later." He sheathed his sword long enough to pull out the clean rags he kept with him at all times. It wasn't his first wound. He tied the bandage, counting the seconds as the mist slowly rolled toward them, licking his dry lips. One last good yank to pull it tight and stave off the bleeding, wincing from the pain as he pulled the sword out, the muscles along his back and arms tensing. "Is there a plan here?"

Leira ignored his question, planting her feet, determined not to go easily, if at all. She looked back and forth between Agnes, the fallen Sirius, Juliana, the few younger Witches and Wizards still standing and the dark mist. It was a lot to stave off and was coming at her from every side. Juliana looked pleased as she braced her arms in the doorway, sure of what was going to come next.

Leira scowled, itching to toss a fireball at Juliana just to wipe the look off her face but she knew better than to split her focus. *Let the Witch think she has the upper hand, for now. Need to come out of this one alive and in this reality.* "Hold them off," she yelled to Lois.

Lois pushed her glasses back up as she whipped her wand back and forth in long sweeping gestures, sending out a continuous stream of small fireballs meant to wound or at least inflict pain. Agnes and Juliana were easily able to fend them off, but it kept them busy. The younger ones among them weren't so lucky and ran howling into the recesses of the building as Lois edged closer.

The mist edged up to the road just yards from Leira giving off a stench that was hard to place as it piled up on itself into a growing tower that billowed out from the sides.

Leira and Louie watched it grow taller till it was at the roofline of the building. Yumfuck let out a growl, pushing out a sound wave but it bounced off the smoke and dispersed to the sides.

"This is new." Leira swallowed and raised her arms. "Time to trust this magic shit like I never have before." She couldn't feel the presence of Mara joining her but pushed the thin worry out of her mind. *Later... There will be a later to ask what happened.*

She opened her arms waiting till the last possible moment to pull off the bracelet. *Rather become light than darkness if that's my choice. At least I will save Louie and Yumfuck. That may have to be enough for me. Let's see how far I can push it before that happens.* "Come on baby, fill me up and let er rip. I can take it." She gently bit her bottom lip, hesitating for just a moment. *I'm sorry Correk.*

She set her shoulders and held out her arms even wider, fingers spread and walked forward. *Better to meet the enemy than cower here, waiting...*

Yumfuck moved with her, staying by her side. She looked up at him, the green hair on his head standing up straight and the fur along his arms bristling. She gave him a nod and a crooked smile. "Thank you, my friend." She looked back at Louie. The noise emanating from the mist was growing louder sounding like a freight train that was gaining speed. "Finish the mission," she yelled to him over the noise.

He opened his mouth to say something but at the last moment, shut it and gave her a sharp nod.

There was nothing left to do but fight. "You've chased me long enough." The glow of the fire threw a blue cast across Leira's face.

The roar from the dark mist grew louder. Leira slipped

the bracelet off her wrist and held it in her hand just as the dense black mist ripped down the middle with a sound like nails down a blackboard, setting Leira's teeth on edge.

Lucius emerged out of the mist, craning his head and beating his chest, letting out an angry howl. He had shifted into the beast easily towering over any of the remaining shifters. A female yipped and quickly ran off through the vines, tearing them as she ran.

Lucius tilted his head back and let out another howl. Leira gripped the bracelet tighter in her hands as she glanced down at her arms. The symbols flashing by on her arm startled her. They went back and forth, torn between warning her of an ally or a foe.

Leira looked up, narrowing her eyes and set an intention even as she still squeezed the artifact, making contact with it. *Set an intention like you never have before.* "Do whatever you have to... I turn it all over to your care." The magic swept up into her legs and surged out from her belly lifting her inches off the ground. The artifact was still making contact with her skin and the light was gathering, circling her even as it pushed out in every direction, surrounding her in light.

Lucius stepped forward, slowly dropping to all fours, the muscles along his back rolling with his movement and the ground shuddering underneath him.

He looked at Leira, tilting his head to the side as she held his gaze.

I will not die gripped by fear and I will make sure you know I was here. Leira's toes grazed the ground. She sent the magic out in front of her, seeing her own brilliant, glowing trail encircling the beast, stirring the fur along the sides.

Lucius shook his head, annoyed and swiped at the trail of energy.

Juliana stepped from the doorway, pleased with how well her plan was working even if the house behind her was slowly becoming engulfed in flames. Sirius was an unintended casualty, but his wounds still might heal, and his death might prove to be an even better outcome for her. The reins of power over the old families were so close.

The sound of lightning crackling split the air and there was the smell of ozone burning as a portal opened to the far side of Lucius near the vines. Mara stepped through, leaping to the ground, her long dark hair falling around her shoulders and her eyes already glowing from the magic coursing through her veins. She was in thigh high leather boots and a long suede tunic. A bow resting in one hand and a quiver of arrows on her back. It was her old clothes from her days on Oriceran.

"I got your distress call, granddaughter. Something about it was different. I came prepared."

"Nana..." Leira arched her back as the energy continued to build within her.

"Sorry it took me so long. I had shoved all the old gear to the back of a closet. Who knew I would need to play fucking warrior again in this lifetime?" She was shouting over the noise.

Mara stood up tall and pulled an arrow out of the quiver, the head a glowing fireball. She pulled back her arm and took stock of the beast. "You..." she hissed. "The fucking beast that tormented the world in between. I should have known you were behind the dark mist. Payback's gonna be a real problem for you. I'll make sure of it. Four years of duck and cover." Mara moved closer to Leira, still aiming the arrow.

The beast let out an angry growl and stood up on his hind legs, ready to pounce.

Yumfuck flexed his arms and let out a howl, determined to get in front of Leira and Mara. But Lucius had other plans.

He turned and ran laterally to the side, toward Juliana in the doorway.

"No, you stupid…" The color drained from Juliana's face as she took a step back and weakly raised her wand, unsure what to do. Lois looked on in horror, wondering if she was about to see her sister in law torn to shreds.

Lucius leapt through the air, easily covering the ground between them, landing neatly just feet from her. "Mine!" he roared, loud enough to be heard. He stood back up on his hind legs and beat his chest. "Vengeance is mine!"

Juliana's eyes grew wide and she turned and fled into the house. Agnes swallowed hard and hovered next to Sirius as Toby pressed himself against a wall. Nothing was turning out the way the clan said it would go. He wanted to run but he couldn't convince his legs to move.

The other Witches and Wizards took off at a run in every direction, deserting Agnes. Juliana reappeared at the doorway, a determined look on her face, her eyes dark with fear and anger as she ran toward Agnes and Sirius, barely edging by Lucius. She waved her wand as she ran, creating a portal low enough to the ground to lift Sirius and push him through as Lucius lumbered toward them.

"Hurry!" yelled Agnes, tugging at Sirius' arm. Leira wanted to follow them. She could see the estate from her vision through the portal, but Lucius blocked the way and was closing in on Juliana.

Mara grabbed Leira by the arm and yelled to Louie. "This is our cue, come on," even as the mist swirled around their ankles. Lois made her way around, joining them. "You too, Yumfuck." Mara hastily opened a portal as Lucius lunged for Juliana.

She had a leg into freedom as his claws gouged her back, catching on the fabric of her cape as he lifted her into the air and slammed her onto the ground. Agnes reached through the portal, pulling her hand back as the beast swiped at her. She watched in horror as Lucius tore at Juliana's flesh and she cried out in pain, lifting her wand to defend herself only to watch her hand rip off at the wrist and fall to the ground, still gripping the wand.

Leira held out her hand to Yumfuck as he shrank down and jumped into her palm while Lois and Mara went through the portal. "The portal's not holding, Louie. There's nothing you can do for her. Not now."

Louie was still standing in the same spot, his sword drawn, unsure what to do. Leira peppered him with pea-sized fireballs shaking him out of his stupor. "Now or never," she growled through clenched teeth. He turned away as the beast finally ripped out Juliana's throat, ending her suffering just as Agnes' portal closed, a look of horror frozen on her face.

"Karma is a fucking bitch," said Louie as he sheathed his sword and ran for the portal, leaping through. Leira followed closely behind him as Lucius turned and lumbered toward her, picking up speed.

"Come on, come on, come on, close already." Leira

stayed by the opening, Yumfuck on her shoulder, ready to defend the opening if necessary, as the portal shrunk down and finally closed, snapping and sparking. She could feel Lucius' hot breath just as it shut. "Too close." She stood perfectly still, not willing to move yet. It took a moment till she realized she was in the middle of the sanctuary in Texas. She fell to her knees, her arms shaking, the bracelet digging into the palm of her hand.

Back at the vineyard, Toby slid down the wall still tucked into the shadows of the building as he watched Lucius roar, blood dripping from his claws. The shifters answered with howls that echoed from the fields.

Toby shook as he peered around the edge of the building. He wanted to see if the end was coming. He held his wand feebly in his hand and watched the mist gather around Lucius, enveloping him in a swirl of darkness and wind till he vanished into it. The loud roar of trains immediately stopped and there was a silence. Even the birds were quiet.

Toby could hear the pounding of his heart. The main house was quickly turning to ashes as the blue flame burned itself out, contained by the spell to the one building. He looked over at the scattered remains of his aunt and turned his head, throwing up the contents of his breakfast. He steadied himself, leaning against the large open doorway to the building, his entire body convulsing as he sank to his knees. "I'm outta here and I'm never coming back. Never..."

Lacey Trader came down the narrow, twisting back stairs hidden inside the Water Tower building, lost in thought. She spotted a young dark-haired wizard heading out the door and called out to him. "Erickson! Agent Forty-Five!"

The agent turned, distracted and looking at his phone. "Lacey! How can I help?" He smiled broadly at her, sliding his phone into his pocket and hiding his distress.

"There's been an all out fight between the dark families and a large pack of shifters. Outside where anyone could see them! We need feet on the ground. Get a squad together and check out the battleground. Remove any signs of magic." Lacey shook her head, still muttering to herself as she went back up the stairs. "Shifters out in the open! Try keeping a lid on magic after that. What's next? Gnomes parading down Broadway?"

Erickson waited until Lacey disappeared around the curve of the stairs and he couldn't hear her anymore. He pulled out his phone and checked the text again, his face convulsing into anger.

No trace. We'll keep looking.

"Dammit! I was this close to capturing that Elven woman and her child." He took a deep breath and let it out slowly, smoothing back his hair. "Revenge will have to wait a little longer," he said, heading out the door for the closest Starbucks. "But I will have it eventually. Someone has to pay."

CHAPTER SIXTEEN

L eira stayed on her knees as Yumfuck sat down on her shoulder, patiently waiting, not saying a word. Mara came over and offered her granddaughter a hand, helping her up. Louie carefully balanced on one leg, the wound pulsing and the bandage he tied soaking through with blood. He gingerly untied it, wincing as the blood trickled down his leg. "Man, that smarts." He felt lightheaded and shut his eyes, willing himself to stay upright. He reached behind to his pouch and pulled out a clean rag, letting the bloody one drop to the ground.

Lois bent over, pushing her glasses up her nose, peering at the wound. "You need to get that looked at. I can take you to someone local who can stitch you up. Fewer questions about deep gashes made by five-inch claws. Here, give me that." Lois wrapped the bandage tight around his leg, whispering a spell the entire time. Louie felt himself relax and even put his hand on her shoulder to balance himself. "Wow... what is that spell? That's better than

Oriceran weed. Still hurts but I suddenly don't care anymore." Louie gave a loopy smile.

Leira rubbed her face with her hands. "Nana, what was that beast? He was twice the size of the other shifters. What did I hear you yell? He created the dark mist and was trapped in the world in between with you... That's fucked up."

"It's a guess but a pretty good one. He ruled the world in between. He was in there for as long as anyone could remember and was known for sucking the essence out of the darker beings that were trapped there." Mara shuddered at the memory. "Awful business. Worse than death. A real life version of zombies but even those things aren't tied to a dark being, doing his bidding."

Leira shut her eyes and made herself listen to the sounds around her. Birds singing, the rustling of the Texas wind through the leaves. Safe and sound. She opened her eyes and looked around, consciously noting the ground underneath her feet.

"I'm gonna get going and take Louie with me before his wound gets much worse." Lois was holding him up as he hopped on one foot. "I'll let Hagan know we're all okay. In the heat of things, I forgot to tell him much of anything. We'll have to work on that one, I suppose. New system, bound to have a few bugs."

"Thank you for coming. I suppose I should be annoyed you put a tracker on me but..."

"I've been doing this sort of thing for a long time. Your grandmother can tell you. We've crossed paths before." Lois nodded to Mara. "Wondered what happened to you. Should have known you were related to this one. I see the resemblance now. She fights just like you do, running at things instead of away from them. Have to admire that."

Lois opened a portal to the inside of a clinic on the east side of Austin. A nurse looked up, unconcerned and turned around to yell to the back. "Looks like we have an injured Wizard. Betty, you're up." An orderly came and helped Louie through the opening and Lois followed him, giving a wave to Leira as the opening snapped shut, sparks falling to the forest floor.

Leira bent over for a moment, putting her hands on her knees as the troll stood up, balancing on her back, still waiting. She breathed in and out and stood back up. "That was a battle."

Mara let out a laugh and patted Leira gently on the back. "That was a good one, but you've already seen worse."

"Not with a possible ending like that one. Usually it's just death." She took a longer look at her grandmother. "Warrior, huh? Don't remember you ever mentioning that one before. How long is your resume?"

"Long enough. I may be a little older than you realize. Don't ask. What's a few hundred years between friends? I was a warrior a very long time ago and hung that up when I had your mother. It was supposed to be my past but then you came along, and the world decided to pull itself apart..."

"And here you are. I kind of dig it."

"We should get going. Might be a good idea for me to change before your mother turns up. Her wedding is right around the corner. How about we don't scare her about what didn't happen till after the honeymoon."

Leira walked toward a clearing. "Deal. I'm telling Correk, though. We promised something about no secrets."

"He's a good one. I see the way he looks at you."

Leira felt her face grow warm and changed the subject. "You ever need to talk about those four years in the world in between, I'll listen. Don't think I ever got what a hell it was till today."

Mara took Leira's hand and opened a portal to the apartment she shared with Eireka, peering through the opening. "No one home, coast is clear. Come on." She stepped through, still holding on to Leira's hand, letting go as the portal closed behind them.

Leira took in the smell of lilacs as she hugged Mara and felt herself relax even further.

"I tell you what, Leira, if I ever get to a place where it's giving me the willies at night, I'll speak up. But, till then, no one else needs to bear those memories too."

"I don't know. There's been more than a few people who keep telling me this is the point of being here. Working together and sharing crap."

"Spoken like a real Berens woman."

Leira's phone buzzed and she pulled it out of her pocket. "Forgot I had this with me. Damn vineyards didn't get any reception and I'm pretty sure one of the spells the Gardener put on the sanctuary was a ban on all technology. Holy crap, I have nine missed calls from Turner Underwood. Mind if we catch up more later?"

"Go be a superhero." Mara rubbed Yumfuck's head as he trilled. "You did good today, my friend. I'm proud of you."

"I don't have my car here. Fuck, he's calling again."

"One more portal, on me. Go, I need to change and stuff this outfit somewhere before your mother turns up. She's a pretty good detective too, you know." Mara formed a ball of light, singing into it and pulling it apart.

"Thanks for showing up, Nana."

"Always and forever, Leira."

Perrom stepped out from the shadows of the forest, the scales along his skin flipping back to honey brown as he watched the last of the portal close. The Gardener emerged from the front of the trees where he had been standing, changing color from the grey of the bark to a deep brown. The vines in his hair coiled around, weaving in and out of his long hair. He could still smell the odor of the beast lingering in the air. "Lucius found them." He shook his head. "He was headstrong when he was a mere Light Elf. The world is pulling itself apart and Lucius may be the tipping point."

"Then we stop him."

"If we can, son. And it better be before the humans find out. That should not be their introduction to magic."

CHAPTER SEVENTEEN

Correk and Leira stood by the open entrance to Hillsdale on top of Enchanted Rock, waiting.

"Strangest family dinner ever." Leira gave Correk a crooked smile. "How does it feel having your dad back in your life?"

"He's not really back in it, not yet. This is the first family thing and the last one was decades ago."

"Wow, that is deep. I suppose we kind of have some things in common after all."

"Not really. Your mother and grandmother were fighting to get back to you."

"So was Harkin in his own way. He may have gotten the details wrong, but he had the same intent. You know, Mara pulled a pretty fast one with my father and my mother may have been mad at her for a while, but she still wants her around." Leira shaded her eyes against the setting sun splashed across a purple and pink sky. "Love a Texas sunset. Where is the Gardener? You think he got lost?"

Correk laughed and felt his shoulders relax. "Maybe it was a mistake having the first family dinner in a kemana."

"No, it's perfect. Where else could we bring your wanted Elven father who's not exactly used to how we do things here? Estelle's?"

"That's where you took me."

"Point taken, but you weren't wanted by the palace guards."

"There are no palace guards. It's just Queen Saria and by now, the king."

"More than enough. Finally." The air sizzled and sparks bounced off nearby rocks as a portal opened from the sanctuary. Harkin stepped through as the Gardener held it open and waited till he was safely on Enchanted Rock. Just as quickly, he let it shut, sparks skittering along the ground.

"Magical of few words." Leira put out her hand to shake as Correk pinched her arm. "Hey! Well, what am I supposed to do? A hug seemed inappropriate and he's your dad, after all."

"And here I thought I'd make things awkward," said Harkin.

"Yeah, what he said. Harkin, we're glad you could make it. My mom and Nana are excited to meet you. Actually, you already know Nana, don't you?" Leira was already heading toward the wide stairs down into the kemana. "Fuck me, the stories you two can tell. I'll bet half the stuff you got in trouble for, my grandmother was there to see it. Hell, Nana probably got away because she can conjure a spell faster than anyone. You were too slow."

Her voice trailed off as she turned a corner, still talking.

"Sometimes she does that when she's nervous and there's no one to arrest or at least chase down," said Correk. "Never mind. Right this way. You're about to see what an underground world of magicals here on Earth looks like."

Harkin followed behind his son, surprised to find himself relaxing, even smiling as they went down the stairs. They wound around and around till they came around the last corner and Harkin stepped into the traffic of magicals around the town square.

His mouth fell open and he gazed up, wide-eyed at the enormous purple-colored crystal stretching up the center and disappearing into the Earth far above their heads.

"Scuse me. Sorry, passing through." A Nicht pushed past him, the bat wings folded on his back and a bag of groceries cradled in his arms.

Harkin looked at them in surprise, his mouth still open.

"What? You look like you've never seen a magical, Light Elf," sniffed the Nicht.

"Come on, Harkin, we're going this way. Leira's already gone ahead." Correk tugged at his father's arm, pulling him along with him down the street to the right, past rows of shops.

Harkin reluctantly followed him, peering into every shop window and commenting on everything he saw. "They have those old candies I used to buy you! Remember? The ones that opened up and had a prize inside of them."

"Don't tell Leira that story. She'll say it's at the root of my junk food addiction."

"Hey, there's a grocer. Look at all of it."

"Harkin come on. Everyone is waiting."

They finally turned a corner and headed down a side street away from the bustling crowds and the shiny storefronts. Harkin picked up speed to keep up, his smile growing as he looked around, taking in everything. "It's like being back on Oriceran. Did you see that sky overhead? Those are Oriceran constellations. That giant rock must have so much magic poured into it to be able to pull that off. Wait! Was that a Willen?" The words spilled out of Harkin as he patted his pockets, making sure he still had a pocket full of pintas.

Correk watched his father taking in the sights like a ten year old.

"It's like he never really got out of prison till just this moment." Leira slid her hand around Correk's arm.

"Yeah, it does look like that. I'm not saying that he didn't do a lot of things wrong, but he paid a price for all of it. Maybe I didn't see how high a price."

Harkin passed by Leira, still commenting on everything he saw. "There's an entire city down here. Does it connect to anything? Do they ever need to go topside? Oh look," he said, grabbing a flier. "There's a Louper tournament."

"No one feed him any sugar tonight. It might put him over the edge," whispered Leira as Correk elbowed her in the ribs. "Just sayin. I've seen you after a family sized bag of Twizzlers. Not pretty my friend."

"Do you remember the last family dinner?" The nearby streetlights blinked and came on, casting a pale yellow glow.

"Do I ever. I gained a father. Hey, there's a theme. Hopefully this time Nana has nothing to confess."

Leira caught up with Harkin and gently took him by the shoulders, stopping him in front of a worn Colonial style house. "We're here."

"This?"

Leira gave a crooked smile. "Yeah, I know it doesn't look like much but it's about the people and not the surroundings. Come on, we're around back."

"It's owned by a Willen family," said Correk, arching an eyebrow. Leira let out a hoot of laughter when she saw Harkin give the same quizzical arch. Correk immediately lowered both of his brows in a scowl, earning another sound of laughter out of Leira.

They walked between the houses down a worn strip of grass and came to the backyard.

"Oh, this is nice," said Harkin, slowly taking it all in.

Floating around the perimeter of the yard were golden luminaries giving off just enough soft light. In the center was a long wooden table covered in a white tablecloth and candles lit down the middle.

"These are my new favorite lights," said Mara, coming to give Leira a hug. "Everything looks wonderful. Harkin!" Mara didn't wait for permission and quickly grabbed him in a tight hug. Harkin stiffened at first and swallowed hard but gave in and wrapped his arms around Mara, leaning into it.

Leira leaned closer to Correk. "Nana has a way of making people choose quickly in social situations. I'll bet that's the first hug he's had in years."

Correk's eyes widened for a moment as he went to put his arm around his father. "Let me introduce you to everyone else, Harkin."

"Well done, Correk," muttered Leira. "I think you just chose grace."

The group gathered around Harkin, all talking at once, smiling at the Light Elf. He was overwhelmed and happy at the same time, not sure what to do.

"I'm Eireka, Leira's mother and this is my boyfriend, Don."

"Good to meet you. Amazing place, isn't it? You should have seen the looks I got walking around here. Like they'd never seen a human before."

"This is my dad, Jackson. He came all this way for a family dinner," said Leira as the troll bounded off the table and crawled up her leg. She scooped him up and put him on her shoulder, still smiling at Correk. "Look, our Dads are talking to each other. How weird is this? Are you getting lightheaded?"

Correk batted away Leira's hand. "I am doing relatively well."

"Everyone grab a seat." Mara clapped her hands and shooed Leira and Correk to the far end to sit near Harkin. Even Yumfuck had a place setting and promptly sat in the middle of it.

Mara waited until everyone was seated and took her place, standing at the head of the table. "First, I'd like to welcome the newest member of our tribe, Harkin. Your son, Correk is family to us, which means now you are too. You will find we are loyal to a fault and are the first to show up when there's a fight or when there's a party. Fortunately, tonight is going to be a party. Welcome Harkin." She raised her glass of wine as everyone else joined her, clinking glasses around the table.

Leira smiled and gave a nod to Harkin just as an acrid smell filled her nose. She jerked her chin to the left, taking in a short breath and glancing around the perimeter, even as she kept smiling. A low fog was curling in around the edges of the worn picket fence.

Leira laid her hand on Correk's arm and leaned toward him to whisper. "Do you smell anything?"

"No, why? What is it?" He felt her energy rolling through his body and out across the yard, seeking a source. Something was off.

The magic circled a mass just entering the property, curling around it and blending with it, side by side. *There's something familiar.*

Leira jerked around, standing up and knocking over her chair. "Fuck me. Wolfstan Humphrey!" she shouted, her eyes aglow and the symbols lighting up along her arms and neck. The fur along the troll's back stood up and he leapt to the ground, growing in size to his eight foot stature.

Harkin jumped to his feet, pulling a short dagger out of his boot as Correk lit a fireball in his hand.

The mist took shape and Wolfstan emerged with a leering smile. "The rumors about you are true, Leira Berens. You have remarkable powers. Harkin, good to see you again and how lovely. A family reunion. So all is at last well. You're more forgiving than I would be, Correk. I don't see the point. I mean, how do you trust after everything that's happened?"

Mara and Jackson came and stood on either side of Leira, their eyes glowing. Eireka remained next to Don, her hand on his shoulder.

"They'll let anyone into a kemana these days." Mara peppered the ground around him with acorn-sized fireballs, backing him up a few steps.

"Mara Berens, I presume." The fog continued to swirl around the lower half of his body as he waved his arms dramatically. "Let me get right to it. I can see that you all have a prior commitment."

"I know what you did to Fraekin," said Harkin, narrowing his gaze and studying his old cellmate. "You won't get away with it."

"I already have. Let's see if you do." Wolfstan's smile turned into a menacing scowl. "I'm not here to break up your meet and greet. This is just a friendly warning. I mean, I got yours. It only seemed right to return the favor, but this time in person." The fog curled higher up his chest. "Get in my way again and I'll consider it an act of war and all bets will be off."

"This has been you being restrained?" Leira felt her energy searching for answers. *Set an intention.* "Stop the bastard," she hissed under her breath.

"Now, now, Leira," growled Wolfstan. "Did you think I would come here alone? Two Jasper Elves? I'd have to be crazy." He narrowed his eyes and lit a ball of light, throwing it into the air. Ringing the property were Kilomeas holding an assortment of swords and longbows. "My usual bodyguards but without the pesky glamour needed up there." He pointed toward the artificial night sky. "You might take me out, but I'm sure I'd get to one… maybe two of you. Which ones do you pick?" He pointed at Mara and then Don with a shrug.

Leira pulled her energy back, just out of range of the

fog. A Willen scurried along behind Wolfstan, pressed close to the fence and blending in under the pale lights.

"I've said my peace. Good luck, Harkin. Trevilsom Prison is a downer in the winter." The fog rose up over his head and a shadow fell across the ground. The Kilomeas retreated from the yard, blending back into the darkness.

Leira could feel her pulse pounding in her ears. "That felt a lot like a limp dick."

"All the frustration, none of the fun," said Mara.

Jackson opened his mouth to say something and thought better of it. "Who was that dick in particular?" he asked.

"Wolfstan Humphrey," said Leira. "A very dangerous Light Elf because he's playing a game of all or nothing."

"My old cell mate from Trevilsom prison." Harkin laid his knife down on the table, clearing his throat. "I feel like I brought this down on the rest of you."

"Not even close, Harkin." Leira shook her head. "He has a master plan that is way bigger than whatever feud he has with you."

"We have no feud. If we did, I'm pretty sure he would have hunted me down a long time ago. Wolfstan doesn't carry a grudge toward anyone. He just kills them."

"Leira's right, Harkin." Correk leaned on the table, anger rising in his chest. "What is the one thing that drove Wolfstan in prison? Trevilsom is supposed to be impossible to survive... unless you have a clear focus on something. What was his?"

"Respect. He felt he never got any. He was seen as an outcast from the time he was born according to him. He swore some day he would make sure everyone respected him."

"I'm not sure he knows the definition of the word," said Leira. There was a tug at her sleeve, and she looked down to see a Willen dressed in a worn black North Face puffy vest. Some of the lining was poking out around the pockets.

The troll leaned over Leira's head, growling down at the Willen who shivered in fear.

"Down Yumfuck. We're on Willen property right now and they've always been our allies." She took the Willen's paw and placed her other hand over it, a hum of magic passing through her. "What is it?"

"I have a trade for you."

"Show me the goods first."

Yumfuck growled again but Leira raised her hand, silencing him. "Back up, Yumfuck. You're drooling on my head, dude. "Come on, Willen. What you got?"

The Willen dug into the folds in his skin, rattling other items already secreted in there, finally pulling out a skeleton key dangling from a gold chain.

"Why would I want this?"

"I know the answer to that." Harkin came closer to get a better look, breathing hard. "I know that key. It belongs to a trader in the Dark Market. Where did you get it?"

"I took it off the disappearing Light Elf just before he popped out of view."

Leira's eyebrows went up and she slowly formed a crooked smile. "You stole from Wolfstan Humphrey..." She grabbed the Willen and kissed the top of his head. "You are a badass. What do you want for it?"

"His pocket watch." The Willen pointed at Harkin, nervously rubbing his paws together.

Harkin bit his lower lip but didn't hesitate. "Take it," he said, pulling out his watch and holding out his other hand for the key. The usual procedure with a Willen.

The Willen dropped the key into Harkin's palm, scooping up the watch at the same time. He gave a slight bow and pushed the watch into the folds, dropping to all fours and running down the side of the house toward the street out front.

"This is not good news for the trader. He'd never give up this key voluntarily. Malek must be dead."

"Why would Wolfstan want that key?" asked Eireka, holding Don's hand.

"It's a trinket," said Leira. "I've seen it before. He must be taking them from his victims. Another soft spot we can capitalize on."

"What's the other one?" asked Jackson.

"His need for respect. I think I know why he's building his empire." Leira stood with her hands on her hips. "He wants a seat at the table. Now, if we can figure out which tables… Oriceran Light Elves, or is it corporate chieftains or maybe the Feds? Once we know that, we can start to take them from him, one at a time."

CHAPTER EIGHTEEN

Leira stepped onto the thick lawn of Turner's estate by Lake Anna and looked around for him but no one was outside. *I'm here*, she texted. "Go play." She held out her hand for the troll as he hopped off her shoulder into her hand and she put him on the ground. "You more than earned it." He ran to the wide leaves of the nearby bushes, rolling in the dirt.

The moon shone over the lake as Leira watched a woman slowly row in a skiff, stretching back and forth.

"There you are." Turner appeared at the side of the house, waving his arm frantically, tapping his cane with his other hand hard against the ground. His mouth was pressed into a thin, agitated line. Leira took one last look at the lake and let out a sigh. "That didn't last long." She ran easily to Turner, grateful for the chance to stretch her legs even for the short distance.

"What's got you all worked up? Too much coffee after five?"

Turner didn't answer her as he turned his back to her and walked briskly across the patio and into the door.

"No Zen words of wisdom? I could use a few right now. Where are we going in such a hurry? I did not even know you could move this fast." Leira picked up the pace. "Geez, I don't think I've eaten all day. Lost my appetite after that dinner." She patted her belly, feeling the familiar sting from the scar. "Now, I know I was in it deep. I forgot about food. May have to stop for a pizza. I wonder if Correk's eaten..." She stopped short at the door to his study, the hunger instantly fading as her mind went momentarily blank and she instinctively pulled in a surge of magic through her feet, her eyes already aglow.

Rhazdon was standing in the study by the window watching the troll play in the moonlight.

"What is that demon bitch from hell doing here? You tried to kill my mother." Leira formed a fireball and lifted it up to throw, rushing toward Rhazdon, who didn't resist or put up her hands. "And you almost killed Correk." The image of Correk lying on the ground flashed through her mind. Turner moved to stand in front of Rhazdon. "Get out of the way." Leira said the words as evenly as she could.

"No... I didn't bring you to my house to kill her. I could have taken care of that myself quite neatly and kept it to myself. I teach you, remember? Put that thing away. Do it." His voice turned icy.

Leira looked at what remained of Rhazdon. She was an old woman, hunched over, the skin grey and sagging on her face. The tentacles were writhing on her head even though they were pulled back into a loose ponytail.

Leira closed her hand around the fireball, not taking

her eyes off Rhazdon. "You caused so much pain for so many people. Killed friends of mine. You deserve to die."

"I would not argue that point," said Rhazdon. "Lucky for you, I don't have a lot of time left either way. The spell to keep me youthful doesn't work like it used to and I'm rapidly catching up to my real age, which means soon I will be dust."

"Not soon enough."

Turner tapped his cane angrily against the floor. "Not in my house! I've trained you better than this. You have to mix the heart with your head, or you will never get close to your real potential." His voice grew louder. "We are entering into tricky times and can't afford to be foolish. You will listen, Leira Berens."

"You trust her? After everything she's done..." Leira shook her head angrily. "No... not this time."

"I trust what she has to say, nothing more and you need to hear it."

Rhazdon sat down on the small couch. "My information is easily checked. I came to tell you how to defeat the shifters."

"You...made...that...beast." Leira struggled to get out the words, choking them out.

"I did all of that, it's true. I cursed him to hell and didn't think of Lucius again." Rhazdon looked up at Leira, resigned. "I wanted to be someone, someone unique." She sat up a little taller, staring into the distance. "After all, I was an Atlantean." A deep sigh escaped her as she shook her head, the tentacles shifting. "I let it all go too far." She looked up at Leira. "Dark magic poisons everything it touches eventually. I thought because I could still manipulate it, I was the exception, but my arrogance grew into cruelty and was the consequence of my hubris. I was a fool."

"We need her help. Remember these words, Leira. Nature does not know right or wrong, *only* consequence. You want to judge her for what she's done and there are scores who would agree with you. Very few who would see any other path. But if we lose the coming battles because of your need to exact some price, can you live with those consequences? I cannot. Let go of the need to change the past. Even my magic can't accomplish that trick. Let the magic show you how to let go."

Leira looked at Turner, confused as he urged her to unclench her fists. He put his hand firmly on her shoulder, squeezing hard. "Revenge in the end will cost all of us more than we can afford to pay. I need you to find the better part of yourself and let it lead."

We aren't in the justice business. That's somebody else's job. We put the pieces together and bring em in. Another Hagan rule. It would have to do. Leira closed her eyes so she couldn't see Rhazdon. Let it start there. I'll have to grow into this one.

"It's like a light switch. You either choose to move on or you don't." Turner's voice floated into her mind overlaying the stream of magic floating through her.

"Have you told her about Tess?" Rhazdon's voice jarred her back into a different reality.

"Not now…"

Leira's eyes popped open. "What about Tess?" The anger returned wrapping itself around the energy stream. "Do you mean the seer who's so famous on Oriceran? Did they find a lost prophecy?" Leira made herself look at Rhazdon. Can't learn anything if I don't look at the suspect. Rhazdon quickly looked down at the twisted knuckles of her aging hands in her lap. Leira's forehead wrinkled as she looked at Turner Underwood. "Ever hear the old saying that an omission is as good as a lie?"

Turner rubbed his weary face with his hands and heaved out a sigh, leaning on his cane. "I have handled this badly. Another sign my days as the Fixer are numbered." He looked Leira straight in the eye, holding her gaze. "Alright, no excuses, no back story other than your word that what I'm about to tell you goes no further. Your word, first. This is too important."

"I tell Correk or no deal and I find out what's going on, on my own. You can count on it."

"Agreed. Tess the seer is still alive and living in a kemana city under Paris."

Leira looked confused. "She's human, that's not possible."

"She has the human spark like you do," said Rhazdon. "The DNA mixes with other DNA and comes out in unpredictable ways like seeing the future, living longer or unheard of magical abilities."

"No, you don't talk. Not to me, not yet... or ever. No..." Leira shook her head. "You kept so much from me and you're my mentor, Turner."

"I have been keeping Tess' secret for hundreds of years. Every Fixer makes that promise. Before you ask, no, Correk doesn't know yet. He will not have the pleasure of a smooth transition like I did. Magic is slowly returning to

Earth and this time technology is in the way and nothing is routine or predictable."

"The shifters... that's your doing. You started this particular string of hell."

Turner sat down heavily in a chair. "Actually, that's not entirely true. Rhazdon is not the creator of dark magic, only a grand master at using it. Things happen in layers over time. Shifters were first brought into being so long ago no one can remember how it started. They hide among us on both worlds already and have for years. Many manage to get up, go to work, have families and fit in right under our noses."

"That's not what I saw at the vineyard. They looked crazed."

"That part is my doing." Rhazdon lifted her chin defiantly.

It reminded Leira of the battle on Enchanted Rock. The losses... Larry... Grandmother Willen... There were so many reasons not to trust this woman. A shifter in her own right who took on many forms.

"I combined two very powerful spells to create shifters who found it difficult to think for themselves." Rhazdon gave an anxious smile. "It seems to have fallen into the wrong hands in my absence."

"You cursed a Light Elf from the royal court and then topped that off by shoving him into the world in between. You set in motion a plot that killed the Prince."

"Yes..." Rhazdon bit her lip, choosing her words carefully. "The curse as you call it. It's why he's out of control. Lucius always did have a strong mind but he's fighting the spell and all those years in the void has turned him into something unexpected that draws in the essence of dark magic like metal to a magnet. They seek each other out and it only makes him stronger and yet, adds to his confusion and his rage."

"I imagine he has a few things to say to you, in particular."

"I imagine I'm the only thing he really wants in any reality you can conjure so that he can finally absorb me into his revenge."

Leira finally took her first full assessment of Rhazdon, forcing herself to push whatever anger she was holding out of the way. "You're hoping he catches you. He's your ticket out of this world."

"No... not yet. I have to reverse some of what I've done, if I can." Rhazdon hung her head. "I was wrong to come after you. Let me do some good in the world before I go. Heed my warnings. The darkness that fills his body seeks out energy and since I no longer have much, it wants you. Learn my knowledge while there's still time. Help the world accept the gates opening."

Two familiar strands of magic came up through the Earth and entwined themselves around Leira, vibrating as they climbed. Leira smelled lilac in the air and felt the gentle nature of her mother, and the fortitude of her grandmother wrapping around her shoulders. They had felt her pain and come to join her, to remind her of what matters in the end. *I asked Correk to forgive Harkin. Not really the same.* Leira felt the anger loosen all the same. "You get one chance with me. One narrow chance and only because so much hangs in the balance."

"Then we had better get started. Removing the darkness from the shifters will not be easy."

"I take it changing them back to average Joe's is off the table."

"That has been tried and usually steals their humanity as well, leaving them as empty shells. The most I can offer is to at least give them back their freedom to choose."

Leira shifted in her leather jacket. *If Nana and Mom can do this...* "Okay... I'm listening."

CHAPTER NINETEEN

Leira listened to as much of Rhazdon's stories as she could stand, long into the night. She paced the room, taking breaks to run around the estate, digesting as much as she could, only to come back and listen to more. Rhazdon laid out her entire sordid life, trying to leave out some details but Leira pressed her for every corner.

On one of the runs she circled the estate again and again as Turner stood at the window, watching her under the moonlight. They were getting to Rhazdon's years as the false prophet and Correk's name came up. Leira bolted for a run leaving Rhazdon in mid-sentence. She lapped the house several times, finally stopping on the back lawn by the lake, leaping over a cement gnome, sweat dripping off the tip of her nose. *I still want revenge. Some taste of it.*

She pulled out her phone to call Hagan and hash it out with him. He might be able to see it as a case, despite everything but she saw the time, four a.m.

"Hello..."

"Correk? Did I wake you?" She had wanted to wait to

tell him. But she knew there was never going to be an easy time. This would wound him deeply. *He was just getting past Harkin reappearing.*

That Rhazdon held the key to anything and they would have to take her help. That was the thing churning inside of Leira. The bitch still had the power to hurt someone Leira cared about and there was nothing she could do to stop it, except tell the truth.

"No…yeah, kind of. I was waiting up, but I must have dozed off. Where are you? Did something happen?"

She heard the concern in his voice followed by a giant yawn and instantly thought of a joke, something to make him laugh, but she bit her lip, hesitating.

"You still there? Hello?"

He should hear it from me. "I'm here at Turner Underwood's place. He has Rhazdon. She showed up to help." Her voice cracked in the middle and she pressed her lips together, determined to let Correk talk it out, but instead there was silence.

For once, she broke one of Hagan's rules and talked first. "Okay, I guess it's my turn. You still there?" *Fuck, caring about someone…* She could feel how fast her heart was beating.

Correk let out the breath he was holding, resting his head in his hand. He sat forward on the couch, trying to figure out what to say.

He thought of his days next to the king. *Stick to the mission when you don't know what else to do.* "Has she given us anything useful?"

Leira's eyes were glistening as she looked up at the stars. "All of it. She's dying and she says she's trying to make things right before that happens. Something cliché about the error of her ways."

"You believe her?"

"Not for a minute. But her intel could help us figure out what the hell is going on and how to get ahead of it before there's some kind of war. I keep picturing shifters running loose, like a bad remake of Werewolf of London but this version would have the army involved. I saw one tear a powerful Witch's throat out. She didn't stand a chance. He was enormous and came walking out of the dark mist. Nana showed up at just the right moment... It was bad."

Silence fell between them and Leira just let it be for a moment. Frogs sang down by the water. "Nana said he was her tormentor in the world in between. That beast or shifter from hell ran the joint."

"Lucius... You're talking about Lucius... He was a friend of my grandfather's. We never knew what happened to him." Correk was making himself take deep, slow breaths, even if his fist was clenched at his side.

"You know about that..."

"Turner told me that much." He looked over at the red velvet chair where Leira always dropped her purse and her blue and orange running shoes, her favorites, one on top of the other by the door. "I can do this. I can do this for the greater good." He pounded his fist on the couch, willing it to be true. "Get what you can out of her. Do something with it that will help as many as possible."

Leira blurted out the words. "I'll walk this with you. We'll face all of this together. I mean..." Her words tripped over each other. *Damn, I didn't know I had this much awkward in me. Too late now, might as well keep going.* "I know we face things together already, but that's just because you were assigned to watch over me." *Get to the point.* "I'll look out for you... because I want to."

"Leira... Leira... my assignment ended a long time ago." He managed to let out a small laugh. "I'm here because I want to be. I'm here because I woke up from almost dying and all I could think of was coming back here to be by you. You can be a little slow on the uptake. You take a fireball to the head?"

She let out a deep breath, relieved. "More like I was standing in the middle of a shifter stampede and lived to tell about it." She looked back up at the stars, trying to remember the constellations of Oriceran. "I meant what I said, I'll walk through this with you. May have to be a slow walk, still not the best at the whole feeling thing but I'll do it. Correk? I wanted to ask her so many questions, to make Rhazdon suffer. But then, I remembered you struggling to forgive Harkin. And I felt my mother's energy and Nana's energy and I was wrapped in it and I couldn't do it. But what she did to you..."

"She didn't succeed. I'm still here and in one piece. Get what you can out of her and we'll compare notes. We should tell the Gardener and Harkin. Perrom thinks the Gardener knows more about shifters than he's telling us. Hell, maybe this will even help Peyton. Come home soon. We'll make a plan."

"There may not be a fast solution. According to Rhazdon, you have to get close to a shifter to remove the darkness and there's that whole fangs and claws thing."

"We'll get everyone to meet at the sanctuary and work out a plan that can adapt when necessary..."

"Probably daily… I should get back in there and get a little more before I take off. Yumfuck was with me but he took off. Said something about cleaning up the streets."

"He is Batfuck… You could have stopped him."

"He can take care of himself. You should have seen him fight today. He is a badass superhero. Wolfstan should be afraid."

"Another problem."

"We'll save that one for another day."

"I'll be here when you get back… unless the Fixer alarm goes off."

"This is a much weirder life than I was anticipating a year ago."

"We're just getting started… Go get what you can and get home."

Leira hung up the phone before she realized she hadn't told Correk everything. *Tess is alive and living under Paris.* She shook her head. "Information overload." Her brain was already swimming from all the information. "There's time to tell him everything. I need a shower, a nap and a breakfast taco. I'm not sure in what order. And I'm talking to myself. Fuck me." She stretched her back and took one last look up at the moon. "I can do this… we can do this."

Yumfuck Tiberius Troll stood on the curb on the East side of Austin in the dim light of a streetlamp wearing his blue cape and mask, slightly worse for wear from the fight at the vineyard. At the last moment he had remembered to gather them up on their way back to the portal. The cape had a rip from a claw, trampled by the shifters as they ran, and the mask was covered in dirt stains. The troll didn't care. "I am Batfuck."

He puffed out his chest and put his hands on his hips, turning in a circle looking for trouble. He jumped onto a nearby parked car and scrambled over the top, landing on the hood to get a better view.

Nothing.

A silver Honda Accord was sliding to a stop next to him and he saw his chance, leaping onto the roof and hanging ten over the edge of the front window, his arms out like he was riding a wave, his cape flying behind him.

The car turned a corner as they passed a Ford Explorer and a sleepy child raised his head in the backseat. "Hey, it's Mighty Mouse! He's real!" The boy pressed his nose up against the glass, turning in his seat as the Honda pulled away from them. The troll spotted the boy and waved, flexing his muscles. "I am Batfuck," he chirped.

"Go back to sleep Joey, you're dreaming."

The Honda drove toward the frontage road to the interstate and Yumfuck leapt onto a passing red truck just in time. He wanted to stay in the neighborhood streets. Better chance of finding a crime to stop. The truck stopped at a convenience store and the troll overheard the driver calling his wife and telling her he'd be home in a few minutes with the diapers.

No action here.

The troll climbed up to the roof of the cab and held on as the truck finally got going again, pulling out of the parking lot. He saw his chance and jumped to a BMW, hooking his claws under the seam of the convertible's roof, making it possible for him to stand up even as the car picked up speed.

But before he could do anything about it, the car easily pulled onto the highway headed north.

"Uh oh..." The troll's cheeks flapped in the wind from the rush of air as he watched the signs fly by. Pflugerville, Round Rock, Georgetown... A semi hauling furniture pulled up behind the BMW, its lights shining directly on Yumfuck who turned and pumped his little arm, startling the tired driver who obliged and pulled the air horn right before he got off at the next exit to sleep for the night. "I am more tired than I thought. My hallucinations are waving at me."

By the time the sun rose, Yumfuck was in Waco at a cattle ranch listening to the lowing of a herd of longhorns. "Damn, wrong outfit. Should have worn my boots. Next time. Aloha motherfuckers!" He waved to the cattle who looked up for a moment and quietly went back to chewing the grass. "Few hiccups but a pretty good start to the crime fighting. Paid a visit to Fleeker, rescued a cat, went on an adventure. Check, check, and check."

CHAPTER TWENTY

Charlie Monaghan sat behind his desk in his home office stewing. No one was taking his calls anymore. His eyes were sunken, and his skin was ashen from a lack of sleep and he was wearing the same shirt from a few days ago. Everything he had so meticulously built was falling apart. The board had held a meeting to make him emeritus and remove all daily duties, stripping him of power. The deal with Fleeker had been the last straw.

They expected a fight, but the blackouts were becoming more frequent and there wasn't much fight left in him. What there was left of his old voracious ambition was focused on holding the bits and pieces of his sanity together.

That wasn't working either, and he knew it.

His wife had left their home along River Road in Richmond and gone to stay with her sister in the Hamptons for a while until Charlie could get his shit together. He roamed the house at night, staring at old photographs taken at political rallies and fundraisers where he was one of the stars.

All gone.

He wandered out of his office and headed for the kitchen, toasting a photo hanging in the hallway of himself and the governor, raising a Waterford glass of two fingers worth of Ragged Branch bourbon. "How the hell did I get here?" He took a healthy swallow and set the glass down on a tall, skinny mahogany table set by the stairs. "Somebody has to still owe me something. I know too much! That has to still be a card I could play. What if I started talking about all the Oriceran food getting ground into people's cornflakes? I can crawl my way back if I have to."

He wrapped his hands around his head and squeezed tight, shutting his eyes. "No, can't let in any distractions. Doctors said there's nothing wrong with me that a vacation couldn't fix." He wiped his sweaty face on the sleeve of his pale blue cotton button down shirt and shook his head, hard. "I'll take a vacation when someone takes my goddamn phone calls!" His shouts echoed in the empty house.

He pulled out his cell phone and dialed Senator Thatcher's office, standing up straighter to get into character. "I can do this. Just like a million other times."

"Senator Thatcher's office."

"Hey, Wendy, it's Charlie Monaghan. Can you put me through?"

There was a slight pause, something new. "The Senator is in with constituents, but I can let him know you called. Was there a message?"

Same kind of bullshit message I tell my secretary to tell

people. It wasn't helping his mood. "You can tell the sumabitch I have a long fucking memory and to put me back on the list of acceptable callers." He hung up before Wendy could answer him in what he knew would be the same even, light tone.

He picked up the glass and threw back the rest of the bourbon and headed back to his office.

The spinning relic still sat on his desk, mocking him. "You! You were the start of my problems. I blame you. Had to go playing with magic."

He rested his fingertips lightly on the edge of the metal, surprised it wasn't sparking or burning his skin. He gave the artifact a gentle spin, listening to the low-pitched moan it gave off as he poured himself more bourbon.

I can make them fear you.

"What?" Charlie looked up, feeling the edge of the darkness coming over him.

It happened a lot lately just before a blackout. He was finding himself in strange places more and more. Standing on a train platform at 126th in New York City during the morning commute or walking down 6th Street in Austin or even standing in the backyard of Senator Allan Kacy's home in Hanover County, staring up at an old oak tree in the middle of the night. The howl of distant wolves startled him out of his stupor that time sending a chill down his spine. *Wolves in Richmond... really?*

You want them to fear you? I can do that for you. Open yourself to me. You can still have it all. No need to settle.

The voice was female, low and soothing, familiar. She had been whispering to him for weeks.

"My only fucking friend is a porn star in my head.

Perfect." He swished the bourbon around in his mouth and swallowed.

Open yourself to me, take back what's rightfully yours. Make them fear you.

Charlie looked out the window at his lawn, still perfect, carefully tended to by the service that came like clockwork. He blinked his eyes, trying to remember what time of day it was and looked down at his wrist, startled to find his favorite watch wasn't resting there. Somehow, that unmoored him most of all.

He looked up at the ceiling. "Yeah, okay, why not? It's been Freaky Friday for some time now. Portals to different worlds. Pointy eared men who can throw a mean fireball. Why not an invisible helper. Sure... go for it. I'm all yours." Charlie distractedly drank down more bourbon, waving his arm. "I mean, what else can I lose at this point?"

The dark mist seeped in from every corner sliding toward Charlie, but it took a moment for him to notice and another for it to register with him that something was wrong. It was the unusual smell that he noticed first. Unpleasant but he couldn't quite put his finger on it.

His eyes turned completely black as the mist crept closer.

"What the fuck?"

He dropped the glass, the crystal banging with a thud and a slight bounce against the thick Persian carpet, rolling onto the wood floor. Charlie's body shook as he sank to his knees, his eyes wide with fear, the darkness creeping up through his veins.

"Not like this..." It was his last words dropping off into a low moan as the dark mist enveloped him completely sucking him into the world in between, leaving behind a damp smell of bourbon on the rug but no other sign of whatever happened to Charlie Monaghan.

Lucius rolled his head to the side, stretching his neck. He was in human form, dressed in the clothes he stole from a house near the Napa estate. He could feel the mist gathering strength from more volunteers who played too long in dark magic and gave in to the call. "A human. Will have to do."

He had gotten used to the draw of energy and was good at telling when the body that was claimed was magical or not.

He smiled, craving a shift into the beast but resisting the urge. The connection to the other side of the veil was strong but there was the mission, still. Hunt down Rhazdon. He could feel her presence in the world.

The dark mist had other plans and was trying to turn his head and get him to search for more energy. Go after Leira Berens. He was happy to oblige but that was second on his agenda. His muscles ached and his skin rippled along his back as he stopped just on the edge of shifting into the animal. "Not right now. Time to do some recon. You'll get what you want, soon enough."

The darkness was like a bad marriage for Lucius that he couldn't quite shake and instead had to make compromises where everyone at least got their piece of hell.

175

CHAPTER TWENTY-ONE

The troll rolled into the guest house after breakfast looking for food, still wearing his cape and mask.

"Whoa there..." Leira picked him and held him out in front of her. "What is that smell? Why do you smell like..." She held him just a little closer to her face. "Is that cow manure? Tell me you weren't tipping cows. That's not nice, you know."

"You can tip a cow?" squeaked the troll, giving her a wink.

"Not exactly an answer. You didn't go anywhere near Wolfstan Humphrey or Fleeker, right?"

"I kept my word."

"We will fight that one together. Geez, how big was that cow?" She carried Yumfuck to the kitchen and pulled out an old plastic bucket from under the sink, filling it with a few inches of warm water and squirting dish soap in it. "Think of this as a bathtub with bubbles. Go for it. There's bacon in it for you afterwards."

"You had me at bacon." The troll dropped the dirty

mask and cape, draping them over the sides and dove headfirst into the water, doing the backstroke around the edge.

"Estelle's making breakfast for me. The woman has some weird radar. She can always tell when I need comfort food. Try scrubbing off some of that while I'm gone. I'll even see if I can wrangle a pancake for you. It's like a flat doughnut..."

Leira went outside and found Correk sitting by himself sipping coffee. Estelle was behind the bar standing on her step stool drying glasses, occasionally glancing backward toward the kitchen.

She came over with another mug and a fresh pot of coffee, setting both down in front of Leira. "Chow will be out in a few. You two take a load off." A cigarette bobbled between her lips as she spoke. She blew a perfect stream of smoke just as the wind picked up, blowing it back around her head. She closed one eye and breathed in deeper, blowing out more smoke as she headed back inside the bar.

"Sure she's not magical?"

"I check all the time," said Correk, pouring coffee into Leira's mug and pushing it toward her. "One hundred percent Texan. Hell, maybe that's its own kind of hellacious magic."

"Mom would agree with that." Leira crossed her legs, trying to figure out how to start. "You okay? Look, I'm not good at checking on others. Not a lot of practice. Hagan will tell you I kind of suck at it. I mean if you're in trouble, or Harkin is in trouble, I know how to run in and do my best but..."

"This is the most you've babbled the entire time I've known you."

Leira gave him a crooked smile. "Yeah, I think we've entered the awkward phase."

"Speak for yourself."

"Yeah? Plenty of past elven conquests? Smooth, and you're an effin liar. You didn't answer me. You doing okay knowing Rhazdon is just across town living in really nice digs with your fearless mentor?"

Correk clenched his jaw and tried to hide it by drinking from his mug but Leira saw it. "I'm making peace with it. It's not the first time I've had to let go of revenge. Probably not the last. The world got more complicated since we fought her on Enchanted Rock and the stakes got higher. I can do something foolish and finally kill the bitch and lose the chance to put down the dark wizarding families before things escalate. Maybe even give away Lucius' chance at getting back his old life…" He fell silent as Leira reached across the table and took his hand, lacing her fingers with his.

"When you put it that way, doesn't seem fair to steal that from him. Despite what he's become, none of this was his idea. You're a good man, Correk."

The gate swung open and Leira quickly pulled her hand back. *Not ready to broadcast to the world.* She felt her face warm as Correk smiled, arching an eyebrow. "Too much PDA?" he whispered.

"Not enough practice." *Still better at battling dark forces than just holding your hand. Not embarrassing at all.* "Like I'm back in eighth grade but I can carry a gun and shoot off fireballs."

"Ah, you do know how to talk dirty."

"This is a surprising side of you. Like finding the good prize in your Crackerjacks. It's a classic snack that came with a prize."

"So much goodness yet to discover."

"I can tell our trash talk is going to consist mostly of trashy food."

"We'll see." Correk held up his hands and quickly made a small ball of light with a storm inside of it, handing it over to Leira.

"Okay... Elven gifts. Better than flowers but why the storm theme."

"Patience..."

Leira held the small orb in the palm of her hand and watched as the storm passed and the Northern Lights shone inside. "Yeah, better than flowers." The ball was slowly pulled apart by the wind still blowing across the patio, the blue and green lights still trailing behind it.

Hagan came through the opening, striding over to the table carrying a familiar pink box. "I figured you could use some of the good stuff after yesterday." He set the box down on the table and looked around for a clean mug. "You think Estelle has any coffee behind the bar? Hang on." He ran behind the bar and was bent over digging around on a shelf when Estelle came out swatting him with a bar towel. Hagan stood up, backing up with his hands out. "Okay, okay. I invaded your territory. Just looking for a mug."

Estelle gave out a disgruntled harrumph and handed him a mug, one hand on her hip as she looked over at Correk and Leira.

"What?" Hagan looked in the same direction but didn't see anything out of the ordinary. "I brought doughnuts. Do I smell bacon? Can I get in on some of that?" He thought for sure he heard Estelle mumble, *some detective* as she went back into the bar.

"Thanks for sending Lois yesterday." Leira looked inside the box and pulled out a chocolate cake doughnut.

"Wish I could have done more. Not used to being back up. Felt kind of weird. Rose says I'll get used to it."

Estelle brought over a large tray that dwarfed her small figure, easily balancing it as she set down three plates, still giving side eye to Hagan. She went back inside without another word.

"Did I do something to her?"

I can be this kind of brave. Leira took Correk's hand and held on, giving Hagan a crooked smile.

Hagan was still rustling around in the box and he looked up with a cruller in his hands, his mouth wide open. "Oh. Ooooh. Huh, well, I'll be. You are still full of surprises, Berens. I suppose this means I lose the bet with Rose and Yumfuck. I swore you'd have to retire first before you'd really notice men. Rose picked a couple years from now. Gotta give it to the small furry one. He said this spring. Ironically, I got to shell out twenty bucks to him... again. Don't ask." Hagan bit down on half the cruller, pleased with himself as Leira gave him a dead fish look.

"There you go. That's the Leira I know. A little hand holding, a menacing look... I get why the red-headed fire-cracker is not too happy with my timing. Figures. It's about my usual. Hey, does anyone know how Yumfuck got my number at home? He left Rose a message. I had to explain to her who was making that high-pitched cackle on our answering machine and what a troll is… Something about a new cape and a mask."

Leira smiled watching her old partner finish chewing one doughnut while he searched for another one.

"Where is Yumfuck anyway? Don't get up, I'll take some of this to him. Pay off my debt." Hagan carried his plate, piling on a couple more doughnuts as he walked away, whistling.

"Most graceful exit ever." Leira had never heard him whistle, even standing in front of the food trucks.

"Pretty bold move on your part, taking my hand like that."

"Meant what I said, Correk. I'll walk this with you. We don't have to fight the world alone anymore. You were right. We are family."

CHAPTER TWENTY-TWO

Perrom sat on the edge of the forest at the sanctuary in Texas enjoying the sunlight on his head, his eyes closed, his face turned toward the sun. He wanted to get back to Oriceran and see Ossonia, needed to, but he took a few more moments to enjoy the quiet by himself. It was still early in the morning and a lot of the residents of the dense woods weren't awake and stirring yet. Only the songbirds were letting everyone know the sun had risen.

Perrom lay back on the grass and let the scales along his body flip over to match the long, green blades, hiding him in plain sight. He took in a deep, easy breath, making the ground look like it was rolling. His mind wandered, thinking of Ossonia's hand in his as a loud, painful screech erupted behind him.

He jerked his head up, some of the scales partially turning, only part of his face becoming visible along the ground. He looked backward in the direction of the forest where the sound erupted. More sounds of sudden movement.

Perrom jumped to his feet, quickly changing appearance back to his normal resting state of honey brown as the irises of his eyes shifted in every direction looking for clues. The tops of the trees were wildly swaying, all in a southern direction.

Away from some danger. It wasn't a typical predator, whatever it was. The normal ones like large cats or a brown bear were under the Gardener's protective spell and didn't hunt within the sanctuary. Something new had found its way inside.

Perrom ran into the depths of the woods, the light quickly fading under the dense canopy, leaping over familiar tree roots and taking shortcuts through the thick underbrush. He knew every square inch as he slid around the base of a tall, wide oak, running his hand along the bark for balance.

Several elk came running at him, their eyes wide with fear, turning at the last moment and running, fleeing away from something. Perrom put out his arms wide, attempting to calm the animals as their hooves thundered dangerously close to him. The calming spell that normally hung over the entire property was being torn to shreds.

Perrom took off running in the direction of the loudest screams, his heart beating hard in his chest. He came along a familiar path and found small trees and bushes pulled up by their roots, broken into pieces, the ground trampled flat. How is this even possible?

The trail had an abrupt beginning as if the menace had appeared out of nowhere, emerging right on that spot.

Portal. Something magical... something fucking powerful found its way past every protection. This is bad.

The Gardener of the Dark Forest was a master practitioner of protection spells. Something or someone had made a mockery of them.

A roar erupted from just yards away down a narrow path by the magnolia trees, their blossoms scattered along the ground with the green, waxy leaves. He slowed down as he heard the cries of a deer, screaming its last and came closer, taking a sharp turn.

There in a clearing created by the large beast covered in fur stood Lucius, tearing at a deer and feasting on all of it. The deer was past caring. Perrom hesitated, shocked more by something invading the grounds of the sanctuary this deep inside of the forest than the sight of a shifter. The layers of spells were supposed to make a feat like this impossible. All of his irises focused on Lucius, studying the shifter, looking for weaknesses.

Biggest fucking shifter I've ever seen.

He wasn't finding them. His mind was running a million miles a minute searching for the best options. Too late to find his father. There wasn't enough time. His father was back on Oriceran.

All the animals had run to another part of the vast sanctuary but at some point they would run out of room. He would have to defend the forest as best he could until the Gardener came on his usual rounds, hours from now.

He stepped back, forming a fireball as his foot stepped down on a stick in the momentary quiet, making a small cracking noise. Lucius looked up from burying his face in his catch, his face bloody. Perrom considered climbing for higher ground but that would draw Lucius closer to the animals.

He held his breath steady, holding the glowing fireball in his open hand as Lucius wiped his mouth on his furry arm, a low rumble coming from his chest. He kept his eyes on Perrom as he flexed one of his large paws, the long claws tipped in deep red. Perrom held his ground, waiting to see what the beast would decide to do next, satisfied with a standoff.

But Lucius dropped the partially eaten carcass and smacked his lips, looking to the right in the direction of the animals the Gardener had worked so hard to preserve. A steely determination came over Perrom and he flung the fireball, knowing it would find its mark.

Lucius growled and batted at the fireball as it whizzed past him just out of his reach and circled back, slamming into his side, knocking the wind out of him and catching some of his fur on fire. The acrid smell of burning hair filled the air around them. Lucius stumbled backward, surprised but didn't fall.

Now it was Perrom's turn to be surprised but he didn't waste a moment worrying about what it meant. That could come later. He formed another fireball in moments, singing into it and hauled it sideways as hard as he could, watching it split apart into hundreds of tiny fireballs, peppering Lucius' fur.

Too many to be able to put out quickly or dodge. Lucius reared his head back and let out a roar, shaking the tree branches over his head. He fell to the ground and rolled as Perrom sent out another volley, singeing the beast, leaving small welts on the bottom of his feet.

Perrom circled, keeping up the barrage. He smelled something strange, noticing the black curling mist that was spreading along the forest floor but there was no time to wonder what that meant. *Maybe I can get him to shift back, come to his senses. At least run the mad dog off. Get the hell out of here the way he came.*

But Lucius had other plans.

He rose to his feet, his entire body trembling, his muscles tense as he made himself stand the small fires still clinging to his fur.

Perrom saw his chance and opened a portal that opened by the ocean in Oriceran where there would be the least number of Elves or Witches nearby. The smell of salt air blew into the forest as Perrom turned to draw Lucius behind him, even as he kept up the stream of fireballs that were now raining down on Lucius from above.

Perrom kept two irises on Lucius, the others scanning the nearby area to make sure his hunch was right. It was all Lucius needed. He dropped back just enough, bending his knees and leapt forward, his claws outstretched, raking Perrom down his left side, and tearing at the muscles in his arm. Perrom stumbled and fell back into the forest, the portal wheezing and sparking. Perrom gasped at the surge of pain and looked up in horror in time to see the portal tear and the world in between exposed.

Hagan sat next to Lois in the warehouse doing his best to read the symbols on the board overhead. "Artifact discovered... artifact stolen... Witch practicing spells in San Fernando... Light Elf fixing a basketball game. That's a new one," he muttered.

Lois absentmindedly pushed her glasses back up her nose. Her head was bent over an iPad reading a report from General Anderson. "Earle is not going to believe this shit." She looked up, surprised. "Forget I said that out loud. Earle doesn't exactly have clearance. Not that I tell him the really juicy stuff. I know the limits. Those I save for Patty."

"You're babbling. It's not a good look. What does the report say? I'm figuring I at least have Earle-level clearance."

Lois pressed her lips together and arched an eyebrow. "Normally, Patty says something like that and I zing her with a tiny little fireball. Seeing as how you're human and old and might tell on me, I'll skip it."

"Much obliged but call me a rat again and I'll figure out how to throw one of those at you."

Lois let out a snort. "Fair enough. The report is about regular citizens, translate humans, seeing larger than average wolves that have been tearing up plants and maybe a few pets. Then disappearing into thin air. Boy, this is not good. I was hoping I'd get to go to my grave without humans finding out about shifters. I believe they call them werewolves."

"You knew all along about shifters?"

"Of course I did," said Lois, insulted. "I was a member of the Silver Griffins, after all." She slid her finger across the screen, scrolling to the next page. "Shifters have been with us since ancient times, long before the last gates were open. But the natives took them as some kind of sign of the devil at first, and then as pure fiction. The magical community on Earth helped perpetuate that myth and we were all hoping to keep it that way. Humans have proven to be testy when they find out some of them were used in spells and turned into hairy beasts with claws and fangs. They tend to burn the rest of us at stakes when they hear that sort of thing."

Hagan kept looking up at the board even as he fumbled around for the bowl of Starburst. Lois conveniently kept waving her wand to move it inches from his reach. "Dragon egg found on farm in Virginia... Artifact... artifact... artifact..." He looked up just in time to see Lois lower her wand. "Hey! Unspoken rule among partners. You don't mess with the food... ever." He jerked his head back toward the scroll crawling across the middle of the room. The annoyance quickly dropped from his face as he waited to see if the same combination of symbols passed in front of him again.

"There it is... sanctuary. You don't think? Is the magic stream keeping an eye on the sanctuaries? What's that symbol mean? Isn't that death... no, something close..."

Lois lowered her iPad and looked up, the color draining from her face. She jumped to her feet, pushing up her glasses as the iPad slid off her lap. "Maim... that's what that means. Rough translation but close enough. Nothing good. Something bad is happening at the sanctuary."

Hagan looked back at the symbols, doing his best to read them. "I thought that place was the magical Fort Knox for animals."

"It's supposed to be. Hell, this is the first time it's shown up on our boards. We need to tell Leira."

"General Anderson sent her on some kind of recon and Correk's out on a Fixer assignment." Hagan stood up and clapped his hands together. "That leaves you and me. Come on, don't shake your head. From the looks of that thing, there's no time to consult with others. That place means a lot to a lot of good people. Beam me up there. Do it!"

"Oh, I am going to get in so much shit if this goes south. Helping a human being go battle something magical in a hidden sanctuary. So much paperwork if you get killed."

"I'll do my best to save you from the paperwork, trust me. Now do it. Come on, chop chop."

Lois looked up at the coordinates one more time and waved her wand, opening a portal just behind the wounded Perrom. His arm was torn at the muscle by his shoulder and he was bleeding badly. Lucius was towering over him, his arm raised to tear out Perrom's throat.

Hagan leaned through the opening of the portal and lifted Perrom in one motion, pulling him into the warehouse. His hands dipped into the black mist partially covering Perrom, clinging to the hairs on his arm as he pulled back. His stomach lurched at the stench as he held up Perrom's head, even as he looked directly in Lucius' eyes.

"Close it! Close it now!" He could feel the swish of wind as Lucius brought down his paw in anger and lunged toward the opening. Lois was ready and whipped her wand across the open space, zipping the portal closed in the nick of time.

Hagan rested Perrom on his desk, pushing everything off the surface and onto the floor as he laid him back. Perrom's body tried to take on the appearance of the desk, instinctively hiding him but the scales fluttered, going back and forth. "Get some bandages or some rags to stop this bleeding." Hagan wasn't waiting for Lois. He pulled off his tie and wrapped it around Perrom's arm just at the shoulder, making a tourniquet. "Come on Wood Elf, stay with us."

Lois came running with the first aid kit shoving it toward Hagan as she raised her wand, mumbling spell after spell trying to find one to stop the bleeding. "Nothing is working!" She shook her head in desperation. "Has to be that damned shifter! There's something about him. Some kind of spell clinging to him that's poisoning everything. We have to find the Gardener. He may know what to do."

"That arm looks bad. If we don't figure out something, he may not be able to keep it."

Lois shook out her arms and waved her wand, opening a portal to Oriceran. "Then we better get moving."

"Not the way I pictured seeing another world for the first time." He gently lifted Perrom off the desk and held him close as the blood soaked through his shirt making an ever-increasing stain. He stepped through the portal and stood in the clearing looking around, waiting for Lois. "How do we find the Gardener?"

"We don't. He'll find us. I just hope we're not too late."

CHAPTER TWENTY-THREE

Yumfuck sat on the back of the couch in the guest house, wearing his red cowboy boots. He was licking his paw and rubbed his paw on his cape, working at the worst of the stains to see if he could make his superhero costume look a little more dignified. It wasn't working. "Meh, will have to do for now. There's work to be done."

He put on the cape and mask and bounded up to the back of the red velvet chair to get a look at himself in the mirror. "Not bad." He dropped his voice into a low grumble and put his hands on his hips. "I am Batfuck. Time to get to work."

He headed out into the neighborhood looking for trouble. The bar was just getting warmed up with the early lunch crowd as Yumfuck waited in the shadows for Estelle to walk back inside. He saw his chance and ran for the knot in the fence that was just his size and leaped through head first, the cape streaming behind him. It snagged on a nail and left him hanging, floating just above the concrete on the other side.

The troll took the opportunity to spread his arms out straight in front of himself and fly momentarily. He let out a satisfied cackle and put his feet down, working the cape off the nail and examining the small new tear it had made. "Price of justice, motherfuckers."

He took off running down Rainey Street searching for trouble and turned on Driskill headed toward the highway frontage road. He was almost to the frontage road when he heard a woman cry for help. He let out a tiny gasp and stopped to listen, trying to figure out where the cry came from.

"Hey! Somebody stop him!"

A wiry man with a scruffy gray beard and long, dirty dark hair came running down the sidewalk toward Yumfuck. Just behind him down the block a woman was yelling, waving her arms, unable to see the five-inch troll on the ground. She was desperately looking around for help. "He has my purse! Help!"

Yumfuck looked up at the rapidly approaching man and saw the grey leather purse he was cradling tightly, close to his chest. The troll made his move and positioned himself in front of the man's right leg, timing his encounter.

"One Mississippi, two Mississippi, three Mississippi... Now!" Just as the toe of the man's worn work boot hit Yumfuck, the troll grew to a foot tall, startling the thief and tripping him. He fell, face first breaking his nose on the concrete, still clutching the purse, knocking himself clean out. Yumfuck quickly shrunk back down and grabbed the purse, holding it over his head as he ran back toward the woman.

"I have got to cut down on the coffee for sure. My doctor was right." The woman watched, mystified with her mouth open as her purse bobbed toward her, as if it was moving on its own.

The troll dropped it at the woman's feet, crawling out from under it and put his hands on his hips. "I am Batfuck," he growled, cackling, sticking out his tiny chest. "At your service."

"Holy shit, the girls will never believe this one. I was saved by a rat wearing a mask and miniature cowboy boots."

Yumfuck took a bow and stood up smiling, showing all his tiny, pointed teeth. "Aloha motherfuckers," he chirped and ran in the direction of home, the tiny cape flapping behind him. He turned the corner and stopped for a moment, surveying the landscape. "Soon, Wolfstan Humphrey, we're coming for you. That will be the real fight and I'll be ready." He bound onto the top of a car rolling toward home, hitching a ride like a tiny roof ornament out to save the day.

The woman cautiously bent down and retrieved her purse, digging out her phone to take a picture of her rescuer but by the time she stood back up again, Yumfuck was gone. "Okay, maybe I need to start drinking wine in the morning instead," she muttered as she dialed 911.

"911, what is your emergency?" The calm operator's voice came on instantly.

"Um, uh…"

"Ma'am are you okay? What's your emergency?"

"Someone tried to mug me."

"Tried ma'am? Are you safe?"

"Um, uh… yes, I am but the thief uh, tripped and knocked himself out. You better hurry." *Better save the whole story for the girls. Worse they'll do is laugh at me. I was saved by a crime-fighting rat from Texas. Holy shit…* "Aloha motherfuckers is right…"

CHAPTER TWENTY-FOUR

Leira stood in the warehouse listening to Hagan and Lois take turns telling her what happened. Twice she started to make a portal and go over to Oriceran herself, but Lois stopped her both times. "I'm telling you, there's no more we can do for now. The Gardener of the Dark Forest found us pretty damn quick and took over from there. He didn't even ask us many questions."

"Just wanted to know who did that to his son. All we could tell him was a shifter from hell. That same beast we saw at the vineyards." Hagan rubbed his face with his hands. "It was not pretty. His arm was practically ripped off his body."

"His name is Lucius. He was a Light Elf but Rhazdon turned him into that hundreds of years ago." Her stomach turned and she swallowed hard. *The bitch has managed to reach out and hurt someone else I care about and still no justice.* Anger crawled up her throat as she clenched her fists at her side. Her eyes glowed momentarily. The energy sensed her desire to do something, but she held back... for now.

"Rhazdon…" Lois said it with a shudder, slowly pushing her glasses back up her nose. "That dark bitch. She crawled off to lick her wounds after Enchanted Rock."

"Yeah, well she crawled back and sought refuge at Turner Underwood's estate."

Hagan sat down heavily behind his desk and slammed his hands on the top. "What the fuck? When did this happen?"

"It's only been a couple of days. She says she's here to make amends. To give us help with the shifters and the dark families."

Hagan's face turned red with anger. "No fucking way. She's no different than every other felon we picked up for years. They lie to get something they want. If it occasionally helps us out, they don't have a problem with that but there's still something they want more."

"I don't disagree with you at all. But Turner Underwood is insisting we let her help. Lucius was his friend…"

Hagan cut off Leira, waving his arm. "His judgment is fucked." He shook his head. "I saw how Rhazdon fought us on Enchanted Rock. There was no shred of decency in her. She was doing battle with us to get her jollies. A magical psychopath. Where's the justice?"

Lois let out a weary sigh. "Justice gets trickier when magic is involved. Not as clear cut."

"It should be," Leira said evenly between clenched teeth. "Hagan… I gave my word that we'd do this Turner's way, for now. He's convinced we need her help to prevent more chaos and more death."

"Then you should share with the Fixer what Lucius has done lately."

"Does the general know?"

"Against my better judgment, I didn't share all the latest news with him. We still work for him and there would have been way too much to explain. Not sure I did the right thing. How the hell did that beast even know how to find the sanctuary?"

"If I had to guess, it's the bionic animals that are being kept there. Lucius is tied to the dark mist, even now that he's out of the world in between."

"I saw that damnable mist. It was swallowing up Perrom. Couldn't scrub the stink off me even after a few showers. Rose even asked me if I was battling demons in hell." He moved his jaw around angrily. Leira had only seen him do that a few times and it was always when a prosecutor told them a case wasn't strong enough to go to trial, even when everyone knew the killer would try again. "I told her I was battling something from hell here on earth. Regretted it the second the words left my mouth."

"The dark mist has an agenda of its own, separate from Lucius. He's lost control of it. He's after Rhazdon."

"We do need the information Rhazdon can give us." Lois stood back from Hagan and Leira, talking softly. "Lucius is the bigger menace right now and there are thousands of shifters in the world. If he could command them..."

Hagan opened and closed his mouth a few times, finally sputtering out, "Command them. Is that even a thing?"

"He's the alpha over all other shifters. Yes, he can lead them if he chooses to."

Leira sat on the edge of her desk. "Then his focus on Rhazdon is useful for more than one reason." She held up her hand. "I know, Lois, I know. We need her and I gave my word."

"But if Lucius catches up with her... and from what I saw of him up close and personal I'd say that's a real possibility... don't expect me to shed a tear. Rhazdon has killed down through the ages."

"I can't believe I'm going to say this," said Leira, "but Lucius is also a victim. One of Rhazdon's victims who spent almost a millennium in the world in between saddled with a curse."

"I remember when I thought a serial killer was the worst thing we'd have to face, Berens. Go to Turner Underwood. Update him on what his house guest has caused now, even indirectly. We'll continue to hold down the fort here. But you better hurry. At some point this will all spill out into the open and the general will find out anyway. He's not a stupid man and he has other resources. If he puts all the pieces together on his own, he's bound to know we knew already and might see that as a betrayal. Can't say I'd blame him."

Leira stood up and gathered her keys. "At some point, we do have to stop making up the rules as we go. Only problem is the game keeps changing."

CHAPTER TWENTY-FIVE

L eira stood at Turner's tall front door, counting to ten before she knocked. *Wouldn't do any good to go in already angry. Save that for five minutes into the visit.* She finally knocked and waited as she listened to approaching footsteps. The hair along the back of her neck stood on end, and she pulled in a little energy, ready for whatever answered the door.

Turner swung the door wide, taking in the glow in her eyes and grimaced, waving her inside. "Has there been a development?"

"Let me use some of your tricks of the trade and just show you."

Turner looked surprised but stopped in the large foyer and waited, patiently. He had one of his favorite canes with him. The hickory cane stained dark with a silver eagle's head on top.

Leira created a transparent ball of light between her hands, rolling it around as she sung into it just as Correk had shown her.

Turner looked slightly annoyed. "I can see Correk is going to be a new kind of Fixer and share a little more than I ever did."

"Correk is different from you in a lot of ways." An image of Perrom appeared, crossing over the worlds. He was unconscious, lying on a pallet in the Gardener's home deep in the forest on Oriceran. His shoulder and arm were heavily bandaged.

"I'm beginning to see that."

"That's a friend of mine, a good one and Correk's best friend. I haven't told him yet..." She felt a pinprick of regret. "But I'm going to the moment he gets back from wherever you sent him. His best friend almost died, torn literally limb from limb by Lucius. Your old friend... cursed by Rhazdon." Leira tilted her head to the side, pressing her lips together. She was doing her best not to say anything she'd have to regret for the next nine hundred years. Too bad the look on her face said it all.

Turner raised his bushy gray eyebrows and leaned on his cane. "You think my old friendship with Lucius, who he was, is clouding my judgment. Fair enough. But you are going to live a long time and fight many battles, even lose some believe it or not. They will come to temper your wisdom. You are a servant of the greater good, Leira Berens. It's in your DNA and comes forward no matter what happens to you."

"Doesn't change that your friend in many ways died a long time ago and has become a menace to that greater good. Or that your house guest put him there."

"That is where you are going to have to loosen up your old definitions if you're going to still do good in this new world order. We are on the edge of very dangerous times. Far more dangerous than optimistic. Magic is returning and it has stirred the bottom of the pot. All kinds of things that stayed comfortably hidden for thousands of years are bubbling to the surface. You know what's on the surface?" He held up his hand. "Human beings and the lifestyle they've grown to accept as fact. But it was a kind of temporary myth all along. I'd like to put off awakening them for as long as possible. If I'm going to do that I'll need your help and taking this curse off the shifters is the first step. The only being willing to help us with that mission is Rhazdon. The only other beings who possess that knowledge are the damned Wizards and Witches who created this cursed mess." His voice was growing in volume, booming through the house. "You can see the dilemma. Serve the short term need for revenge, which you handily call justice or hold back, serve the greater good on this new playing field and see what apocalypse we might be able to stave off."

"I gave you my word I'd play things out your way. Asking me to like it is going too far. It's not justice, no matter what reasons you come up with. That's the really strange thing about justice, after all. You do it because it's the right thing to do and not because you can't think of a thousand good arguments to look the other way. It's the thing that really stops the chaos at the door. Everything else is what we're going to tell ourselves because we're afraid of this new world order."

"You think I should die." Rhazdon hobbled into the foyer, pointing a twisted, mottled finger at Leira.

"I was wondering when you'd finally barge into our

conversation. I'm not after your death, necessarily. I think you should answer for what you've done. Be made to stand up and tell the entire rabid story to all the victims' families till they're satisfied. Not just share a few spells. But that's just me."

"Rhazdon, leave us. I have business to discuss with Leira that doesn't concern you."

"Like she can't eavesdrop if she wanted to."

Rhazdon turned back at the door, eyeing Leira. "My powers are not what they once were. Neither is my resolve. I have no great conquests to fulfill."

"Save it. You're getting what you want. Selling me on it is a waste of everyone's time."

Turner waited for Rhazdon to go down the hall before he led Leira outside to the slate patio in the back. "I don't entirely disagree with you, but I can't let my emotions run the show."

"Mine aren't. Cold, hard reason," said Leira, tapping the side of her head. She let out an angry sigh. "You wanted to talk to me about something."

"I hope that someday you come to understand why I've taken this path with Rhazdon. Either way, it had to be done. The same reasons are going to pull you away from your job with the federal government. You need to be more independent, able to make the right choices without having to choose sides."

"Like now."

"I'm not asking you to choose a particular side. I'm asking you to use your common sense and utilize a valuable and rare resource against a darker foe." Turner made his way over to his favorite green Adirondack chair overlooking the lake and settled into it. He took a soft plaid wool blanket off the foot stool and threw it over his legs. "Cool day for so late into spring. This is one of my favorite spots in all the world, and I have seen all the world has to offer. Maybe it's because very little changes here."

Leira sat down on the edge of the chair next to him. She zipped her leather jacket up part of the way against the chilly wind. She looked out over the lake and made herself take a deep breath and let it out. "The only reason I haven't dragged her ass back to Oriceran and thrown her down in front of the queen is because of you. Remember that was my original assignment? I was hired by the king and queen to find the person who killed their son. That would be justice."

Turner shifted in his chair. "On that, we agree. It's unfortunate that events changed so much since then and justice will take a backseat to survival." Turner crossed his hands over his chest. "Consider becoming independent. The world has changed, and this will only increase and become harder to handle as the years go by and magic increases. Imagine what the world might be like in say, twenty years."

"Hard to do from here."

"There are written stories about what it was like the last time the gates were opening. It was chaos for a while, and that was before human beings became so advanced in technology. It was a lot easier then to make up some cockamamie story about magic and get the masses to believe. Not going to be so easy this time."

"And everyone wants a little power of their own."

"Yes," Turner said, wearily. "Another complication. We

need someone who can stand in the middle of all the competing forces and choose what's best for the greatest number."

"You mean me. Isn't that vigilante justice?"

"It can be in the wrong hands. It would not be easy, but I believe it is doable and may keep us all from a venomous tipping point."

"You're usually more Zen about the world."

"And I may be again but I'm also a realist. Can't be the Fixer without a healthy dose of that. I can see that the balance is shifting constantly and threatens everyone. We need someone who can be more impartial and cares about…"

"Justice…"

"That's one word for it."

"The dark syndicate needs to be stopped. They're a threat. Wolfstan Humphrey and Fleeker are the greatest threat."

"Completely agree."

"And Lucius is a problem… along with the shifters."

"Different kind of problem. They have a right to exist. Think about it Leira. We all fear them because they seem to be more animal than human or Elf or Wizard. But they're a thinking being. They are not something to hunt down and exterminate. Besides, they've been here a long time, and many have learned to assimilate. Do you propose ferreting them out of their middle class lives?"

"What about the ones who carry the curse?"

"That's where Rhazdon becomes useful. She is the originator of the curse. Darkly ingenious, really. Create a killing machine that can shift into something that can hide in plain sight… and make it connect to you magically. Your thoughts and desires become their motivation, your vengeance their focused mission."

Leira looked up, narrowing her eyes as certain pieces of the puzzle fell into place. "That's it. That's how the dark mist got hold of Lucius. He didn't create it. It already existed and came looking for him. The darkness was drawn to the curse and found that hole inside of his will created by Rhazdon and filled it. The curse makes beings susceptible to the strongest magic around them."

"Remove the curse."

"Drive back the mist. It loses its physical embodiment… for now. Might even make it possible to crush it."

"Especially if Lucius has a two-way street with the mist. If he can tell us more about it than we can know from the outside, looking in."

"Did you see that all along?"

"Not all along. Consider my offer. I have a foundation I run that is well funded for when the day came that life on Earth began to change. I believe it's here. I can give you a new base of operation in one of my safe houses. A rather nice house in Georgetown along the Potomac River. It will come with a very generous allowance. You would be able to buy whatever you needed to get the job done, travel the old fashioned way… in planes, and have visitors." He gave a sidelong glance at Leira.

"Okay, I get it. You're a crafty old dude who can see the obvious."

"Correk is a good choice…"

"Don't make it creepy by saying you approve. Look, I'll think about it. Less than a year ago I was a homicide detective living a pretty normal existence even if I thought my mother was crazy and my grandmother was MIA. It had a certain order to it. Not much changed, and that was the way I liked it. Everything is different, including me. Now, I'm supposed to pick up and move away and do what? Hunt for problems to solve?"

"Trouble will find you. You'll find the house is very well equipped with whatever enhanced technology you'll need."

"You mean like the virtual board at the warehouse."

"That's a child's toy. There are far more efficient ways to monitor the world, and a team of contractors you can call on to help you when needed."

"My own Justice League."

"Don't get ahead of yourself. They're only there for support. They can't ride out to take care of things for you. Do you accept?"

"I'll think about it. That's all I can offer right now. I'll let you know. I'll see myself out." Leira walked around the outside of the house, grateful to avoid seeing Rhazdon again.

Rhazdon watched from an upstairs window as Leira climbed into the green Mustang and drove away down the long driveway. "All I wanted was to be respected and instead I became feared and reviled," she muttered, lost in memories. "Perhaps it's not too late, still."

CHAPTER TWENTY-SIX

"In memory of my beautiful wife." Sirius Pickering raised his glass in a toast. The 2010 Spring Mountain Vineyard Cabernet Sauvignon was a deep ruby color in the firelight in front of the oversized stone hearth. The other elders joined him and raised their glasses. "To Juliana..."

Sirius swirled the wine around in his mouth, doing his best to get the image of the remains of his wife's body out of his mind. That's all there was by the time he got to her. *Remains.*

"Such a powerful Witch and she never got to use her wand. What kind of monster..." The Wizard caught the cold steady gaze of Sirius as his voice trailed off and he took another sip of the wine, choosing to stay silent.

"The beast was on her before she had a chance." Agnes gripped the stem of her glass tightly. "You weren't there. There was nothing any of us could do."

"No one is blaming you, Agnes." Sirius eyed her coolly, swirling the wine in his glass. "At least, not for that..." He tapped his finger against the glass as everyone else looked away, not willing to be involved in his wrath.

"I did exactly as you asked. The trap was set perfectly. That bitch, Leira Berens walked right into it with only a boy Wizard at her side. A thief who calls himself a scavenger. The shifters were set loose on them. If the plan failed, blame their handlers, not me."

Sirius set his glass down on the mantle, warming his hands in front of the fire. "Merely a setback. The curse worked... to a degree. The shifters were unable to think for themselves as a pack. It's unfortunate that one of them slipped the ties that bind and appointed himself the alpha. Interesting though, isn't it? They chose to listen to one of their own."

Agnes took another long gulp, staring down at the carpet.

"Something has to be done about the growing threat of humans and magic. The gates are opening whether we like it or not," said a balding Wizard. "We need to secure our stature. The damn humans have turned out to be a little more clever than we realized."

"The young amongst us show mixed promise at best. Most of them ran at the first sign of trouble. So much for testing them," said a pinched-face Witch with long, straight dark hair. "I knew it would fail."

"Perhaps it's time to vote on leadership roles. We never had a proper council meeting since your brother was dragged into... well, into the world in between." The tall, wiry Wizard with a thick head of dark hair, slicked back gazed down his nose at Sirius. "We need some reassurance that any of our plans will actually succeed."

Sirius looked bored as he raised his wand and flicked it toward the heavy closed doors to the library where they were gathered. They opened softly as five young Wizards entered and stood in front of the door, grim faced and waiting.

"What's this?" The balding Wizard's voice rose in concern.

"Sirius? I demand an answer."

"Is this protection for us? We are perfectly capable of taking care of ourselves."

"I think I'm leaving. Where's my wrap? Are they going to get out of our way?"

Sirius flicked the wand again as if he was leading an orchestra, yanking the various wands out of their hiding places from each of his guests and throwing them into the fire. All except Agnes. They watched in horror as the flames turned a burnished yellow, blue and purple, releasing the magic into the atmosphere.

"What the fuck?" Agnes slowly backed away from the group, relieved she was being spared.

"Come stand by my side, would you?" Agnes quickly did as she was told as Sirius gave a nod to the young cadre of Wizards. They stepped forward as Sirius waved his wand again, whispering a spell binding the other guests' arms to their sides. "You know, feedback is so useful at times. It gives clarity about what to do next. I agree that we need shifters who will feel some kind of natural connection to the families." He shrugged. "It'll make for an interesting experiment at least. Mix it up a little."

The tall Wizard's face grew pale as he tried to struggle.

"No! No, Sirius, you can't! My family has been in this syndicate for almost a thousand years!"

Agnes watched silently, afraid to say anything.

"And the rest of your family will remain. Think of the contribution you'll be making. Who knows? If we're successful this time you can be on the cutting edge of a new form of leadership."

Their screams of protest could be heard all the way down the great hall as they were dragged away. "Maybe you'll even turn out to be an alpha, although I doubt it." Sirius let out a bored laugh as he flicked his wand again, shutting the doors. "Meeting adjourned. More wine, Agnes?"

"Why did you spare me?" she asked, lifting her chin, defiantly.

"Don't annoy me, Agnes. I can call them back if necessary. Drink your wine. You live to fight another day... for now."

CHAPTER TWENTY-SEVEN

Correk stood on the grounds of Turner's old estate in Charlottesville. He was dropping off a reluctant teenage Wizard in baggy jeans and an old AC/DC t-shirt who was being hunted by the Silver Griffins. "It's here or Trevilsom Prison. You choose."

The teenager looked around at the large manor set back from the road and the iron gates. "Doesn't look like much. Is this some kind of juvey hall? I have rights, you know."

"You have plenty of them. You turned over most of them when you decided to send snakes down the main street of your small town."

The young Wizard smiled, showing braces across his teeth. "I'm a regular Pied Piper, right?"

"I think you mean St. Patrick, and no, you're no saint, Joey. You're not even Irish."

"Got that right. One hundred percent American Wizard. See? My underwear is the stars and stripes." The teenager lifted his shirt to show Correk his boxers that were drifting out of his pants. Correk rolled his eyes and took the kid by his arm, roughly moving him along the long driveway toward the house.

"Hey! Isn't this some kind of kidnapping? That has to be against your Fixer rules."

"Your parents were the ones that shoved you at me. Remember?"

"Well, I can't stay here forever. What is this place anyway? Looks abandoned. I'm not gonna be here all alone, am I?" Joey was quickly losing his bravado as his feet tried to run backwards. Correk easily lifted him off his feet, letting him run in air as he half carried him toward their destination.

"You're in luck. The old Fixer has made a deal with the Feds. You are looking at a brand new school for misfit toys like yourself. Seems that some human beings want to be ahead of the curve and they actually think your sorry skinny ass is part of the answer."

"Really?" Joey settled down, giving in and walking toward the manor still in the distance, looking around at the grounds. "Not much here. They'll have to do a better job of jazzing up the place if they want a bunch of magical Witches and Wizards to hang around the place and not set it on fire." Joey threw up his hands to protect his head. "Not that I would do something like that. I know where to draw the line."

"Won't just be Witches and Wizards, Joey. You're going to have to learn to get along with all kinds of magical beings. All of you getting ready to help with the gates opening."

"Ah, the great migration. I've heard about that. Heard my parents talking about it. They think Oriceran is going to pull a Krypton and go boom." He blew out his cheeks and held up his hands.

"That's not really the prophesy... they got it wrong... never mind. Drop it. Look Joey, there are spells protecting this place and you'll be able to stay here without being detected. There's a warrant out by the Silver Griffins to take you in to be tried and probably convicted. It doesn't look good for you. You want a second chance? This is it. Keep your head down, do a close approximation of what you're told and try to make something of yourself. You clearly have some talent... Some... You can learn to channel it."

"For the Feds..." Joey rolled his eyes, even as Correk was still dragging him along by his arm. "For the humans who run the Feds. That's like turning on my own kind. Is this really all such a good idea?"

"We're almost there, Joey. Let me know if you want to go with Plan B and we'll step back out on the road where your presence will light up the board at the Silver Griffins nearest headquarters. Shouldn't take them long to swoop down in their minivan and pick you up. Who knows? Maybe they'll set you loose again while you still have hair. Although, if you end up in Trevilsom you may not have enough of a mind left to know if you still have hair."

"School for the human Feds it is. You know if this place gets Wi-Fi? So far I only have two bars."

"Give me that."

Correk left Joey with the groundskeeper who answered the door. "We've been expecting you, Joey. Follow me." Joey gave Correk a look like he was ready to bolt but all Correk had to do was step out of the way and let him.

"Go ahead. Make a break for it. Look out for any soccer moms in minivans while you're out there."

Joey let out a defeated growl and picked up his duffel bag, trudging along behind the groundskeeper.

"See you around, Joey."

Joey responded by slowly raising his middle finger behind his back, never turning back around as he smiled at the groundskeeper.

"Joey will be just fine. He's already learned to smile up." Correk took a last look around at the marble inlaid floors and the vaulted cupola in the ceiling and let out a low whistle as he walked out, shutting the door behind him. "Hope Turner knows what he's doing, setting a bunch of spoiled teenagers with wands loose in his country palace."

He headed for the road, glad to not be dragging Joey along with him. He saw a shadow come over where he was walking and looked up in time to see a young gargoyle come in for a landing, settling on his shoulder, weighing him down. "Two moons, what the hell!"

The gargoyle dug in with his claws, gently pinching Correk's skin under his jacket. Correk struggled to get the gargoyle to land somewhere else but all it did was get the creature to flap his wings longer, batting Correk in the head and stirring up the air around them.

What the hell is happening?

'I know you.'

Correk stopped twisting and turning. *I could swear I heard you speak... inside my head.*

'You'd be right. Remember me? You dropped me off here. I remember you. We're friends.'

"You're a telepath."

'Most gargoyles are. It's what makes us great at working the postal system. We know what you meant to say.'

"How is that helpful?" Correk looked around the grounds but couldn't see anyone. *I look like I'm talking to myself.*

'Then just think it to yourself. I'll hear it.'

That's disturbing. Fly out here where I can see you. Correk pointed to the ground in front of him as the gargoyle reluctantly agreed and lifted off his shoulder, pressing down with its powerful legs.

Correk looked at the winged creature, trying to keep his thoughts to a minimum.

'That won't work. We get intention. I've been waiting for you to come back. I want to blow this joint.'

"You've been hanging out with the troubled youth, I take it."

'Not a nice bunch, believe it or not. One of them tried to fly me like a kite.'

"I believe it, but I can't take you with me. I'm heading out there where magic is still hidden. You'll stick out like a sore thumb."

'Not so fast.' The gargoyle shimmered as the molecules shifted in the air and he reshaped himself into a small corgi. *'I hear these dogs are popular.'*

"How the hell did you do that?"

'Not that hard. Watch this.' The air shimmered again and

the small corgi shifted into a parrot. The bird took flight and landed on his shoulder. *'I'm the perfect companion. Besides, knowing intentions can be helpful.'*

"I don't want a sidekick."

'Think of me as a useful tool.'

"The answer's no. You have a home here. A good home."

The bird took off from Correk's shoulder and shifted back into a gargoyle landing in the road just ahead of him. He stared at Correk, waiting for a reprieve but the best he got was one arched and annoyed eyebrow. *'Fine, for now. But this isn't over. You could use an assistant like me.'*

The gargoyle took flight over the treetops, settling down near the edge of the estate, watching Correk walk out onto the road. *'Soon enough...'*

CHAPTER TWENTY-EIGHT

Louie jumped back through the portal from Oriceran, a few new trinkets in his pockets, his sword safely on his back. He jumped into the living room of the condo General Anderson was providing for him, happy to have a home again. It was government issue basic but still better than what he was used to in his makeshift cabin on Oriceran.

Be prepared. The sword whispered in his ear.

His senses went on high alert and he let the portal close and turned on the lights, swinging around with his sword out, his lip curled into a sneer.

"Relax, scavenger." Leira was sitting in his favorite recliner, her legs crossed, waiting for him in the dark.

"Good way to get yourself killed! What the hell are you doing here? Is there a mission?" He blew the air out of his lungs, puffing out his cheeks as he put his sword back in its sheath.

"I thought you had given up scavenging. Don't bother to lie. That will make things worse."

"I believe you decided for me. I never agreed. Look, it's in my nature. I see something pretty that's just lying around, I want it. Just knowing there's a lot of pretty things left out there lying around is hard to resist."

"Resisting temptation is not exactly in your nature, either."

Louie gave a crooked smile. "Not exactly, no. Besides, had to check on Ronnie. I'm the little guy's best friend. Not cool to neglect friendships." He went to the refrigerator and looked inside for a cold Shiner Bock. "Have you tried these? So much better than that swill at the Rusty Bucket in the Dark Forest."

"I came to tell you I don't need your services anymore. I'm making a… a career change. Heading out on my own."

Louie stopped the bottle halfway to his lips but took a long swallow anyway. "Heading out on your own in a family band? Heading out on your own to discover the world? That's a pretty broad statement." He took a seat on the blue couch that had seen better days and sagged to one side.

Leira sat up on the edge of the seat, resting her arms on her knees. "When we started this little arrangement, things were actually simpler, believe it or not. There were artifacts popping up everywhere and human beings trying to grab them first. Pretty straightforward. I still had a job to do and despite finding out I'm a Jasper Elf, I'm still a Texan. That overrules anything."

"Interesting rule book."

"Things have changed."

"I suppose you're referring to big bad Lucius. That's right, I heard about his name, even his background. Good guy cursed to magic hell. That kind of thing is the best kind of gossip. It's all they're talking about in the Dark Market. Shifters are the hot topic. There's even a rumor that Rhazdon has resurfaced. That one true?"

Leira gave him her best dead fish look, not saying anything.

"I'll take that as a non-committal, committal. That is very interesting. Then there's the rumor Harkin is alive. Yeah, that rumor is out too. Probably because Wolfstan Humphrey leaked it." He leaned back on the couch, crossing his foot over his knee, the small artifacts he found shifting in the pouch still tied around his waist. "Your plate is full of baddies. I can see where something like that would put a different perspective on things. You tell Jackson?"

"Leave my father out of it. Fuck it, leave my family out of it. This isn't an explanation, only a goodbye."

"Appreciate you not ghosting me. Anderson might have cut me loose without warning and I hear the Silver Griffins are still a little hot about a few unauthorized trips to this side of things." His pouch clinked as he moved. "These are all Oriceran, still up for grabs."

Leira got up to go. "I wish you well. You're not a bad guy. Frankly, you fought really well back at the vineyards. It would have been a lot worse without you. You showed up outside of the house at just the right moment. A minute longer..."

Louie thought about the book in the library. *All about the choices we make.* "Hey, here's a crazy idea. Let me join you. Come on, don't roll your eyes. You're gonna need backup and it can't come from a human. They're not equipped for all this. You need someone who's not only magical but has a few street smarts and has been tested in battle. I have fought off my fair share of Kilomeas, angry gnomes, and slimy things I don't even know the name for." He held out his hands, the beer in one of them, shrugging his shoulders. "What do you say?"

"Thanks anyway. Not what I had planned."

Louie quickly set down the beer and blocked her path. "Come on, none of this was what you had planned, right? Not what I had planned. More of the same unplanned shit is coming our way. I have skills you can use. Give me a shot and if it doesn't work, like I end up dead or something, then we part ways. No harm, a little foul."

"You're not good at taking no for an answer."

"I suck at it. Women find it charming. Young ones anyway."

"Call me old again asshole and see how well this goes for you."

"Wasn't referring to you. See you more as gender neutral."

Leira glared at him but started laughing, despite her convictions. "Fine, a trial period that I will probably regret."

"You won't, I swear. Are we staying in Austin? Do I need to find a new place to live? I mean, this place isn't much but the bed's not bad, as long as you don't mind rolling toward the center."

"Stop talking. We're relocating to DC. Soon. Be ready. You fuck up at all and you're out, Louie. That includes disappearing on scavenging trips without notice. You do that, don't come back."

"Got it, done. Partners."

"No, not partners. Not sure what we are, but not part-ners. You take orders from me. We go out there and see if we can hold off mass chaos just a little longer."

"Sounds like fun. Me and my sword are all in."

CHAPTER TWENTY-NINE

Leira slipped in through the side gate as a cheer went up from the bar. "Leira!"

Estelle snapped a towel at Craig and Mike sitting closest to her from where she stood behind the bar. "How many times have I told you not to do that?"

"More times than I can count." Mike let out a laugh and jumped out of the way before Estelle could land another one on him.

"Good one, Estelle," said Cassidy, picking up her iced tea to keep it out of harm's way.

Estelle took out her cigarette and blew a perfect trio of O's as she watched Leira give a wave and keep walking for the guest house. She squinted her eyes through the smoke and grabbed two bottles of beer, easily popping off the tops as she jumped down from her box and walked across the patio.

"I think Estelle is shrinking."

"Shhhh, Scott, if she hears you..." said Mitzi, as she slipped a piece of cheese to Lemon, sitting by her stool.

"One of these days we're going to look over at the bar and all we'll see is a red bouffant and a cloud of smoke." Kimberly smiled and gave Lemon a little of her watermelon.

"That's all I can see now if I'm sitting on the patio."

Estelle turned back to stare down the regulars who all quickly swiveled on their stools, facing the bar again. She let out a deep raspy laugh and turned back to the guest house, putting on another quick coat of her favorite deep red lipstick.

She gave a soft rap and waited for Leira to open the door just wide enough to see who it was, with Estelle holding up the beers. Leira knew better than to try and talk Estelle out of coming in and opened the door wide, while waving behind her back at the troll to go find someplace else to be. She heard a loud tsk as he reluctantly let go of the remote and scrambled for the pantry in the kitchen.

"Might as well settle down in the discount cheese puffs container for the duration," he squeaked.

Leira kept her eyes on Estelle hoping she didn't hear a thing as she came inside. "Something on your mind?"

Estelle looked around for a place to stub out her cigarette, leaving it in her mouth even as it became more ash than cigarette. Leira caught on and went into the kitchen to grab a mug to act as a makeshift ashtray. She glanced in the pantry and saw Yumfuck plastered against the inside of the large plastic container. Most of his fur was already tinged in orange and he was busy licking the orange dust off the inside. "Remind me to tell Correk to not eat whatever you leave," she whispered.

The troll cackled and gave her a wink. "Like I'll leave

some. Good one!" he squeaked.

At the last moment, Leira grabbed a damp washcloth and draped it over the opening of the container. She headed back for the living room already seeing tiny orange paw prints dotted here and there. "How did he do that so fast?" She turned on the radio that sat on a nearby shelf and turned it low to hide the smacking sounds coming from the pantry and kept walking.

Estelle had a thing about cigarette butts on the ground. She dropped what was left into the mug and slid an unlit cigarette into her mouth before completely walking into the living room, keeping her own rule about not smoking in the guest house. It was all out of respect for Leira so she would know this was her home.

Estelle handed over one of the beers and sat down on the couch, as she took a long, slow swig, the unlit cigarette still dangling from the corner of her mouth.

"That'll do." Estelle tapped her cigarette on the edge of the mug out of habit, deftly holding the beer in the same hand, putting it back in her mouth. "You want to tell me what's going on?" She leveled her gaze at Leira, not blinking or looking away.

How the fuck does she do that? "How did you know?"

"Not hard, dearie. You have tells, if anyone would bother to watch. What's going on? You look like you have the weight of the world on your shoulders."

"That's probably a little overstated." She paused, looking around the guest house. *My home for the past four years.* "I got a new job offer. But it's in DC."

Estelle chewed on the end of the cigarette, making it bobble in her mouth. "Is it a good job?"

"It's a great opportunity to do some good." *That's not a lie.*

"So, we're talking a move, here. Out of Texas and into foreign territory."

"Not sure I'd classify Washington, DC as foreign."

"Not Texas and it's a company town and the company is politics, and the politics change every few years, and so do the people. And it's not Texas."

Leira gave her a crooked smile. "Well, when you put it like that."

"I can see you've already made up your mind."

Leira felt a sense of relief come over her. Estelle was right. She had made up her mind to go. But leaving was harder than she expected it to be. "I just found some kind of roots, my roots. Put together some kind of family. Everyone's in a good place. Makes it hard to go."

"Found a good man, who's easy on the eyes." Estelle slapped her knee and leaned closer. "It should be hard to go, little lady. I'd be worried about you if it was easy and you just left me a note on the counter. Your family is here, and I'm including myself and all those people at the bar who don't seem to have anything better to do with their day, God bless them."

"I'll come back to see you…"

"Of course you will."

"And I'll miss this place." She looked around at the tiny room. "So much happened inside these walls. Some of it was the best times of my life." The bracelet slid down her wrist as she twisted the sapphire ring on her finger.

"Oh honey, this is still your home. Hell, this was storage before you came along. This place will always be here just for you as your home. That's not changing as long as I'm alive."

Leira leaned in, risking a snappy rebuke. "Just how old are you?" *Are you part Elf, have you been around for a few hundred years? Are you some kind of alien?*

Estelle winked and smiled as the cigarette pointed up toward her nose. "That's a mystery lost to time. Better if it's kept right there, too. Let's just say, you have a home in the great state of Texas where you can always come home and find the people that love you and know you best. Take that worry off your plate. Go out into the world and put the bo-back-slappyass on the bad guys. I'll sleep better at night knowing you're out there." She put her hand gently on Leira's knee. "And when you need a reminder, you come back here and we'll sit at the bar and talk about bowling, or Barton Creek, and share a little brisket."

"It's a deal." She leaned over and wrapped her arms around Estelle's small, bony shoulders, hugging her close, breathing in the smell of tobacco and Shalimar. "Thank you for everything."

"Wasn't nothing, dear. It's what you do for family. Better get back outside before those regulars of mine start serving themselves and pestering the wait staff. We have a bowling practice to get to. Need to defend our title!"

Leira saw Estelle to the door and went into the kitchen to find the troll sitting on the edge of the table, wrapped in the cloth. There were smears of orange on every surface except on the troll. *He kind of got the point.*

"We're moving?" He was sitting very still, waiting for an answer.

"We are." Didn't think how this would affect the tiny dude. "You okay with that?"

"Hagan coming too?"

Leira hesitated but answered him quietly. "No, buddy, he's going to stay back here in Austin, but we'll stay in touch. Same with Mom and Nana."

"What about Correk?"

"That's an interesting question. Don't exactly have an answer for that one yet."

He held out his tiny paw and Leira held out her hand as he stepped into her palm. "This is part of life. Everything changes, even if you're trying not to evolve, and standing still is not in your nature," he squeaked. "Thank goodness."

"You're like a tiny little Yoda of my very own who eats an amazing amount."

Yumfuck cackled, leaning back in her hand, his paws behind his head. "It takes far more courage to walk forward than it does to stand still, even when it's for the best reasons. But then you find out that the world is a pretty good place to hang out. Onto the next adventure out there. What kind of food do they have in DC?"

"That's a good question. I have no idea. We'll find out together."

"Let's get this part straight. Do they have bacon, Cheetos and Dr. Pepper?"

"Yes, that much I can guarantee."

"Then we're good. We can figure out the rest."

"I like a little dude with priorities."

The troll let out a soft trill. "Yumfuck hits the road!"

CHAPTER THIRTY

Leira knocked on the familiar bungalow, standing back, waiting for Hagan to answer. She came with a hot pizza from Home Slice, extra pepperoni just the way Hagan liked it. She was hoping that would make breaking the news a little easier. The troll was tucked in her pocket with his own piece of pepperoni. He was trying to make it last but finished it in three bites, peeking out of her pocket at the box.

Leira knocked again and peered through glass panes in the front door as Hagan came barreling down the stairs, his shirt only partially tucked in and his hair in disarray. He opened the door with one large pull, sweeping his hand to the side, not saying anything.

"You don't look so hot. You okay? Brought pizza." Leira took in the deep circles under his eyes and the puffy cheeks as she found her way to the kitchen, setting down the pizza. The troll squirmed his way out of Leira's pocket, jumping onto the kitchen island and lifting the lid to the box, breathing in deeply.

Leira ignored Yumfuck and kept watching Hagan. *Something is off. I recognize that look from long stakeouts when we were looking for someone really bad. He hasn't slept.*

Hagan followed her, moving around the kitchen, making tea and setting out a tray, still not saying anything. He was lost in thought. Leira put her hand on his arm to get him to stand still for a moment. She waited till he looked her in the eye. "What's going on?"

Hagan's shoulders sagged and he looked down for a moment, blowing out a breath as he put his hands on his hips. "It's Rose," he said quietly. "Something's wrong. We thought it was the flu at first, but the doctors say it's her heart. She caught something and it traveled to her heart. We didn't know it was happening." His voice broke as he got out the last words. He looked up at Leira, his eyes shining. "I can't lose Rose."

Yumfuck poked his head out of the box, the remains of a pizza slice in his hand and a smear of grease across his face. He dropped the slice and stepped out of the box, looking from Leira to Hagan.

Hagan tried to manage a smile. "You know it's bad when Yumfuck puts down greasy food to listen. I really must look bad."

"What can they do for her?" Leira found a dish towel and wiped off the troll's face, putting him up on her shoulder.

"Damn doctors said to make her comfortable. Talk to hospice. They're giving up…" he hissed through his teeth. "I'll be damned if I give up that easy." An idea came over him and he became animated, waggling his fingers in the air. "Can you pull off some kind of magic thing? Make her better?"

"I have no idea but I'm willing to try." She squeezed his hand. "What if we pool the resources?" *Fuck me, if Rhazdon turns out to hold the answer...* "Can Rose be moved? I say we take her to the sanctuary and ask the Gardener of the Dark Forest."

"What about that hellion, Rhazdon? I hate to even say it out loud, but she knows so much magic."

"Dark magic. She's well versed in how to twist someone into something unrecognizable. Not so much in repairing things. But the Gardener is the opposite."

"Isn't he more of a veterinarian at best? I mean, not that I'm unwilling but..."

"He's the best practitioner of the healing arts that I know of and has trained himself in healing organic matter. I don't think it matters what species. Worth asking and after that rescue you pulled off with his son..."

"Would have done that either way." Hagan shook his head, waving his hand in the air. "No question. Wasn't trying to bargain for something."

Leira gave a crooked smile to her old friend and partner. *A good cop to the end.* "I know, it's just who you are. The Gardener is kind of mythical when it comes to helping the outside world. You, though, will be an exception. Come on, I'll help you get Rose ready. We can carry her through a portal."

"What happened to the rule about using magic on Earth and especially portals? Don't need the Silver Griffins on our tail."

"Fuck the rules." Leira followed Hagan down the hall

and up the stairs.

Hagan looked back at her with a surprised expression. "That's new."

"Okay, I still get off on rules but let's say I'm catching on that every group has their own set. Not going to be able to follow them all. It's a new world. May have to come up with some of my own and near the top of the list is going to be, I don't let loved ones suffer in order to keep any of the other rules. Fuck that philosophy. I'm coming up with my own rules. Next rule is fuck the other rules. I'm going to *rewrite justice*."

"I like this idea. Leira 2.0 with the gloves off. Look out world."

"Probably past due. Stop fighting magical demons with worn out rules made up by others." Leira stepped into the bedroom and saw Rose propped up with pillows, breathing oxygen from a mask. Rose looked up at Leira with the same kind, brown eyes and held out her hand. Leira took it, gently squeezing.

She pulled in energy through her feet, letting her eyes glow and the symbols appearing along her arms as Rose's eyes widened in surprise. She sent a ribbon of magic energy through Rose, setting an intention and watched her skin pink up.

Leira felt the connection and pulled back. Rose's heart could only take so much energy.

"What is it? Why are you stopping?" Hagan paced at the end of the bed.

"It's not working. I'm not fixing her heart, just making it work harder to keep up. I could easily overtax her. Come on, on to plan B."

CHAPTER THIRTY-ONE

Leira and Hagan helped Rose swing her feet over the edge of the bed and slipped a robe around her shoulders. Hagan gingerly held his wife up as he sat next to her on the bed.

Leira stepped back and formed a ball of light in her hands, opening a portal to the Texas sanctuary, relieved to see it was deep inside the forest, making it easier to find the Gardener.

Hagan easily lifted the small frame of his wife and stepped through the portal as Rose craned her neck to look all around her in wonder. Leira picked up the oxygen tank and stepped through after them. Yumfuck bounced along on her shoulder, holding on to her collar.

Leira reached up and plucked him off, putting him on the ground but he wouldn't move.

"It's alright. We'll make sure to take care of Rose. You can go play. You haven't been outside in a while."

But the troll stood right where he was, crossing his arms and steadily gazing at Rose.

Hagan took his handkerchief out of his back pocket and blew his nose. "Will you look at that? He doesn't want to leave. Yumfuck you are worth every bit of money I've spent on you and then some. Next box of doughnuts is on me... again... and you can even have first pick."

Leira gave up and put the troll back on her shoulder as she felt the bracelet warm on her wrist. The bionic animals were nearby, she could sense it. The Gardener was hopefully not far behind.

There was a loud rustling in a dense stand of old growth trees and Leira waited to see an old bull or an elk with bionic parts. She could feel the connection growing as the animal drew closer.

A figure emerged from the depths as the scales along Perrom's body flipped over from browns and dark greens to honey brown. "Perrom! You're better!" Leira felt a relief and went to hug him as he pulled back turning his left side away from her. Leira pulled back, surprised and felt the connection with him even before her hand touched his shoulder. A look of confusion passed quickly across her face. "The connection is with you."

Perrom took a step away from her, a cold, angry look in his eyes. That's when Leira saw his other shoulder. What was left of his arm was connected to his body by a reformed artifact. *A magical prosthesis. I'm connected to you.*

Perrom wouldn't look Leira in the eye and instead focused on Rose and Hagan. "Why are you here?" There was a cold edge to his voice that Leira had never heard before.

"Rose is sick," said Leira, but Perrom continued to look away from her. "We were hoping your father could help."

"My father is not a doctor," Perrom said, bitterly.

Leira could feel the anger inside of Perrom, passing through her. *He feels lost. Your father saved your arm.* Perrom suddenly looked up at her, balling his hand into a fist. Leira held her place as the troll's fur ruffled and he stood up on Leira's shoulder. *Please don't make me defend myself against you... because I will.*

"Enough..." The deep, loud baritone of the Gardener of the Dark Forest rang out as birds took to flight, disturbing the calm of the forest. "Felix Hagan is always welcome in my sanctuaries." The Gardener walked next to a large moose, his hand resting on the large animal's neck. The vines in his long dreads wove themselves around, pulling his hair off his shoulders as small blue flowers opened and shut.

The Gardener was holding a small chipmunk in the palm of his hand as the small creature vibrated with fear. "He's not fond of visitors." The Gardener stroked the small animal's back, putting him down under a large fern. He quickly ran away, searching for a hole into his burrow.

"They're looking for a miracle," Perrom spit out, glaring at Leira.

"We're looking for a way to help Rose live," said Leira, softly. *My patience has limits, Perrom. Zip it or find somewhere else to be.*

"Miracles are what we say when we can't explain things. Let me take a look." The Gardener held out his hand to Rose who reluctantly reciprocated.

Leira noticed Rose was already standing taller as the Gardener sang out to the forest and a yellow beetle answered, landing on his hand and walking quickly over to Rose.

"Ow!" Rose tried to pull her hand back as the beetle stung her. Hagan pushed against the Gardener without success, who still bore the same expression of stern mixed with calm. He shielded the beetle from Hagan before he could squash it as the bug released its venom into Rose.

"The beetle is sharing its gifts with you." The Gardener smiled, something rare as he looked at Rose. "Take off the mask. You don't need it here. Help her."

Rose cautiously reached up as Hagan helped her get the mask off her face and she tentatively breathed in the deep, cool air of the forest. She blinked, looking around, taking another breath, half expecting to feel the crushing weight in her chest again at any moment. But there was nothing.

"I can breathe. How is that possible?"

"Is she cured?" Hagan was anxious and hopeful, all at once.

"Cure I cannot do. The yellow beetle is from Oriceran and it helps align your system to the rhythm of magic. The magic takes on some of the load of working to keep you alive. It's the same theory behind why some magical beings live so long. Magic does some of the work."

"What does that mean for Rose?"

Leira spoke slowly, wondering if she had done the right thing bringing Rose to the sanctuary. "It means she will live as long as she stays here. The sanctuary is now working to keep Rose alive."

"But that won't work. I have my garden and the book club, and all my friends. I can't stay here." Rose looked from face to face for another explanation.

The Gardener shrugged and let go of Rose's hand as the beetle flew away. "You can always leave. You're not a prisoner here. Nothing that lives here is held captive." The Gardener gave a side glance at his son. "But you will return quickly to your former state. There is nothing I can do to fix your heart. It's one of the most complicated parts of any being. I suppose that's good and bad news."

"What do we do now? I had no idea this was a one-way trip." Hagan swore softly under his breath. "I'm sorry, Rose."

Rose took in another deep breath just as the sun broke through the canopy in rays that touched her face. She shut her eyes and felt the warmth against her skin, smiling. She tilted her chin down and opened her eyes in time to see a doe leading her fawn across a path and butterflies lifting off a forsythia bush. "This place... it's not where I expected to live out my golden years. But it's like a little Eden." She gave the Gardener a hard stare. "Provided there's a roof that goes over our heads." She quickly smiled, her eyes shining as the Gardener smiled broadly back at her.

Two times he's smiled in one day. That's your miracle. Leira shook her head. *The world is changing all around me.* "Rule number two. Roll with what is," she said.

"Another good one, Berens," said Hagan.

"There's a small cottage that's been empty for a while. You can live there for as long as you like." The Gardener gave a gentle nudge to the moose, sending him off at a trot as he followed behind him. Not bothering to beckon anyone else to follow.

"That's his way of saying, walk this way." Leira held out

her hand in the direction of the Gardener even as Perrom hung back.

"I suppose I can commute to work from here."

"You can even work from here." The Gardener was going deeper into the forest into places Leira had never seen before. "We aren't all Pixies and Elves in the sanctuaries. You'll find I adapted to reality and life on this world more than others would have guessed."

The hike took them down winding paths with Perrom following at a short distance from the rear. At one juncture where the path split in two directions the Gardener chose a third direction and walked straight toward a thicket, only to pass easily through it. "A glamour..." Leira marveled at the spell, taking Rose's hand as they pushed forward.

On the other side stood a long, low building with a thatched roof. "Don't be fooled by the simple surroundings." The Gardener led them inside the building, only to reveal a room hardwired with technology and screens at a table down the middle. Hagan's eyes widened as he rushed toward the nearest end of the table, looking from screen to screen.

"You're monitoring the world from here." Hagan's voice was full of awe. "This is like the warehouse but raised to a whole new level."

The Gardener stood back by the door, near his son even as Perrom moved away from him.

"He put all of this in after the beast broke through the protection..." Perrom's voice trailed off and Leira felt the ache pass through her chest from Perrom, sending a pulse through the scar on her belly. She saw the anguish flicker on the Gardener's face.

"I should be getting back. Hagan are you okay staying here?" Leira put her hands in her back pockets, watching Rose look out the window toward the gardens in the back and Hagan resisting the urge to press any buttons. *This might just work.*

Rose smiled as Hagan kept moving, not hearing what Leira said. "We'll be fine. I'll make a list of things to bring from the house. That would make this easier." She went to the door and stepped outside as Hagan reluctantly followed her.

"This is all moving a little fast for me," said Hagan.

Rose took his hand. "It's okay, Felix. We'll do this together, like we've done everything else."

"I don't get how you can just give in so easily. This morning we were happily in a life we love…"

"We weren't… not really. That life was quickly slipping away. I mean, I liked our old life… a lot." There was a wistful tone to her voice. She crossed her arms, determined to find the good. "But the old life was being taken from us, and according to some pretty decent doctors, pretty quickly. I'm sorry, I don't mean to sound like I'm struggling to be grateful. What do I call you, is it Gardener?"

"That will do. My given name has been lost to time and another life, and no longer suits me. Gardener will do."

Perrom opened and shut his mouth a few times, trying to find the words. Leira felt the beginning of a shift inside of him. *Rose has her own kind of magic. Things work out the way they're supposed to. Another Hagan rule. Make that my rule number three.*

"I suppose I could see this as a chance to have a bigger garden... Grow a few flowers."

Yumfuck saw his chance and leapt from Leira's shoulder to Rose, landing neatly on her arm and scrambling up to her shoulder. She let out a short *whoop*, and held still, looking at Hagan as he rolled his eyes.

The troll leaned in, whispering something in Rose's ear as a smile spread across her face and she broke out in laughter. Yumfuck smiled and cackled, running back down her arm, leaping into the air, sailing across the distance back to Leira's shoulder.

"Consider that done," said Rose.

"What did he ask you?" Hagan felt some of the tension leave his body. All he wanted in the world was for Rose to be happy. It made it possible for him to do anything else.

"Sew him a new mask and a cape. Something in blue. I'll tell you what. I'll make you a few. Maybe a nice gold, and a red one." Rose shook her head. "I suppose dying is just as weird and that was going to be my next stop. You have to let go of everything you know whether you like it or not. Making a superhero costume for a..."

"Batfuck," chirped the troll, puffing out his chest, his hands on his hips.

"Sure, okay, yeah... So, I landed in a kind of heaven with a lot of weird mixed in. Where's this cottage? Leira can you make sure I get my sewing machine? I'm assuming there's some kind of electricity around here. Which way do we go?"

Leira hung back as the Gardener and the Dryad led

them down a path further into the forest. "So that's your mother." She grabbed Perrom by the arm, his new arm, feeling the energy course through her veins. "I'm glad you survived. It's the only thing I can think of to say. I'm not sorry your father found a way to help you come out of this as some kind of whole being."

Perrom worked his new shoulder, a soft hum Leira didn't notice before breaking the stillness of the forest. "He didn't give me a choice. By the time I woke up, it was already done, and I haven't had the courage to tell him to rip it off."

Leira held out her wrist with the bracelet on it. "I have my own kind of addition. I know it's not the same but there's a similarity. I didn't ask for any of this. The light could absorb me into nothingness. The dark energy is hunting me like I'm some kind of prey. There are different sides all seeking to stake their claim on this world. Some of them have better intentions but I'm not sure anyone has the right to be called virtuous."

"What do you do with the new rules?"

"Break every fucking one till I figure out which ones are still mine and follow those till they don't and make up some new ones. Repeat."

"Tell Correk for me."

"You'll tell him yourself, when you're ready. You'll tell Ossonia too. Correk told me. She'll understand all of it. Give her a chance."

"I don't understand it."

"Okay, she'll get it enough to stay. To stay by your side. That's the point, anyway."

CHAPTER THIRTY-TWO

L eira met Correk out on Rainey Street just as the bars were warming up and the college students were out in force, moving in and out of the bars like a constant stream of ants. On nights like this Leira's nickname for the street was *ant hill*. She looked out over the sea of heads bobbing along the street and smiled as she saw Correk in the middle of the crowd.

She was leaning against the green Mustang as he came down the street. He was dressed in his cowboy boots that were getting worn in nicely, jeans and an ATX t-shirt. *He looks like he's from Austin, just in time for me to drag him somewhere else. If he'll go...* "I am going to have to get used to awkward as a state of being. Fuck me." She put the smile back on her face despite the butterflies in the pit of her stomach.

"I got your message from Turner. He said something about you not wanting to meet there. You two on the outs?" Correk took her hand and kissed the top of her head. Leira resisted the urge to look around and see who might have noticed.

"You barely flinched. Well done, Berens," he said, smiling.

"It's not that I don't like it. It'll take practice. We're not on the outs, exactly. I don't need to have his house guest in my face. I have a better day when I don't have to look at Rhazdon. Can we go for a walk?"

Correk stopped in the middle of the sidewalk as people moved around them, some of them giving him the side eye.

"This is the exact opposite of walking, Correk."

"Tell me what's gone wrong, then I'll walk. I want to see your face when you tell me."

Leira leaned back, her face breaking into a crooked smile. "Wow… that says a lot about our relationship." A shudder went through her. "Sorry, that was involuntary. Not used to being someone's girlfriend. Girlfriend." She pressed her palm against her stomach. "You're still not moving. I suppose if I told you to sit down first, you'd assume I was dying. Or worse, Costco was closing."

"Something like that."

"Well, you can dial it back. It could be good news, you know."

"Is it?"

"Depends on how you take it. First, there's still Sam's Club. Same deal, hardly know the difference and Costco's not going anywhere." She pulled on his hand. "You're still not budging."

"You *still* haven't told me. Spill it."

"I got offered a kind of new job."

"Not really telling me anything. What's a kind of job?"

"The kind that Turner Underwood offers that makes me more of an independent..." Leira shook her head. "I don't really have a name for it, yet."

"Maverick. You're searching for the word maverick."

Leira made a face, considering the word. "I like it. Independent, make my own rules." Leira pulled on his hand again as they walked down the sidewalk. "At last, you're moving, which is ironic because this means I'd be moving. The setup is in Washington, DC. Georgetown to be exact. Fuck, my hands are sweating." She wiped her hand on her jeans and grabbed Correk's hand again. "Not usually this nervous. It's a good central location in some kind of mansion that Turner owns. That dude has got to be worth millions. Is that a normal Fixer thing? And it's near Wolfstan's personal offices. Fuck, I'm babbling." Her stomach did a flip as she got to the hard part. *Still rather run down a felon, clink of handcuffs.* "And I'm hoping that means you'll move..."

Correk stopped on the sidewalk again as a man ran right into him. "Hey! A little warning." The man threw up his hands and walked around them as Correk took Leira's face in his hands.

"Okay, we're doing this?" Leira felt her stomach flip again. *Sound of handcuffs, easy confessions... fuck it...just go with it Berens.* She stood on her toes and kissed Correk. "Fuck who sees us."

"Stop swearing for just a minute, Berens. Or in your case, talking." Correk kissed her back and Leira felt the same surge of energy pulse through her, circling around Correk. She pulled back, smiling, her face flushed and warm.

A couple of fraternity brothers walked out of Icenhauer's bar, tipsy from happy hour. "Alright, alright, alright. Now, that's a kiss."

"Fuckin-A. They're glowing!"

Leira smiled, digging her free hand into her coat pocket. "I don't suppose they're really Elves in disguise."

"No, better. Drunk human males. They'll never remember."

"I meant what I said. I want you to come with me. Shack up with me again, but this time in the same room." She smiled, squeezing his hand but noticed he wasn't smiling. "Am I going too fast?" The smile faded from her face.

"Leira, you and I are both going to live to be hundreds of years old. Don't make a joke, Berens. Let me finish. I've got at least a hundred years on you already."

"You're not robbing the cradle. I'm old in human terms to just be figuring out how to date."

"Had to make a joke. Elves are different than human beings. We find someone and give our heart away and it's like that for life. For hundreds of years."

"I get that. I can do the math."

"Be sure of what you're asking because there's no turning back."

Leira laced her fingers with Correk's, finally taking a deep breath. "It's too late. It has been for a while. It just took me some time to get that. Come with me and we'll figure out the rest." She leaned her head on his shoulder as they walked.

"Fuckin-A," he whispered, kissing the top of her head.

"You know just what to say, Fixer. Better than flowers."

"Or pizza."

"Now I really am flattered."

"Just as long as you never call me Bert again."

Leira let out a laugh, picking up her head. "Deal. Wow, that feels like that was a lifetime ago. You know, Rhazdon being back means I didn't exactly finish the Queen's mission."

"I know it does. We're going to have to figure that one out as we go."

"I get that. Will take a new rule. I'm all about that. Rule number five. Save the world first, settle old scores later."

CHAPTER THIRTY-THREE

Leira woke up to the sound of her phone buzzing on her nightstand. She looked over at Correk sleeping soundly next to her and felt her heart race all over again. His skin felt warm pressed against her hip in the darkness. She was barely able to make out his form under the comforter in the small dark room.

The bedroom was pitch black from the blanket she had hung over the bedroom window earlier to make sure no light escaped. Correk had laughed and said, "No pressure." But she had been right as the shadows of their forms intertwining had played along the walls.

The blanket had worked like a charm, not letting out any of the ethereal light.

The phone buzzed again as she kissed Correk's bare shoulder and picked up her phone, flipping it over as she looked at the clock. *Three a.m. No good news comes at three fucking a.m.* The number was blocked. *General Anderson. I suppose I owe him one last mission, especially since I haven't told him, yet.*

"Hello, sir. What's happened?"

Correk stirred in his sleep, opening his eyes and sitting up. Leira put her finger to her lips as she listened.

"Nothing good," said the general. "There's some kind of confrontation brewing in the heart of Paris. This may be the night we lose the battle to keep magic a secret."

Leira pressed the phone harder against her ear as a shudder passed down her spine. She knew instantly who it was and what they were after. The dark wizarding families. They were making their move to gain real power. The prize was Tess, the seer. *Damn.*

"We don't have any kind of official permission from the French, but I'm sending you in anyway, along with a few PDF agents. They've got a head start on you. I can have a plane waiting..."

"No need. I can get myself there. Can you text me the coordinates?"

"Already done. Check your phone. There are reports of Wizards facing off against some new menace. Sounded like they were describing werewolves. Now, that's just a myth, right?"

"I'll let you know, sir. Let me get to the area and see what's happening." She hung up the phone and checked the coordinates, holding the phone up for Correk to take a look. "Do you know these coordinates? Is this the kemana in Paris? If it is, we have a shit storm that's about to rain down on us." Leira was already rolling out of bed, searching in the darkness for her underwear and jeans.

She banged her shin on the dresser, swearing as she fumbled for a light. Her phone buzzed again as she zipped up her pants, looking at the caller ID. It was Turner Underwood. She slid her finger across the screen as she grabbed a shirt. "We already know. They're after Tess. We're on our way."

"It's worse than that. Someone who knew her secret has betrayed her to the dark families."

Leira stopped getting dressed for a moment as Correk pulled on his boots.

"You mean Lucius, don't you? Man, he is the gift that keeps on giving. Lucius is playing both sides and somehow he knew all along where Tess was hiding. Tell me Rhazdon didn't have something to do with this, too."

There was silence on the other end for a moment. Leira pressed her lips together, willing herself not to say anything more. *Justice my ass.*

"She says she didn't."

Leira ignored him, moving faster as she balanced the phone under her chin. "Turner, we'll do the best we can to stop it before things get even worse. Worse like shifters tearing apart a few hundred innocent bystanders, or even one average human being minding their own business. We have to go if we're gonna make it on time." She hung up without waiting for an answer.

"That was a lot of *we*, you were throwing around." Correk pulled a thin sweater over his head, pulling out his long silver hair as it fell down his back.

"Fuck it, he might as well get used to it. There's a *we* now. Come on, those agents are walking into something they're not prepared to handle and won't survive."

"Lucius must have had a plan all along."

"Clearly," said Leira, forming a ball of light between her hands. "The question is still what his end game is, and I

MARTHA CARR & MICHAEL ANDERLE

don't think it's to help out the dark families so it's hard to say who's walking into the trap. Maybe all of us." Leira sang the coordinates into the light, opening a portal as she pulled her hands apart, making it larger. "Grab Yumfuck. We're going to need him."

Correk opened the bedroom door and found the troll standing on the arm of the couch in his cowboy boots, ready to go. Correk leaned down and grabbed his bow and quiver leaning against the wall. "Leave the boots this time, Yumfuck. By our honor…"

"We shall be known," squeaked the troll, kicking off the boots as he leapt into Correk's hand. Correk walked quickly toward the portal, stepping through onto a Parisian street with Leira right behind him.

"I set us down a few blocks away to give us cover. Figured we would need to see who's already arrived and what side they're playing for before we dive into the battle."

Leira whipped around at the sound of gunfire and screams as Correk set Yumfuck down. "Sounds like we're late."

The troll grew to his full measure, standing up at eight feet tall, claws bared as they made their way toward the sounds of a battle already underway. They turned the corner at the end of the long street just as people were running toward them, fleeing from something. The small knot of people took one look at Yumfuck and veered to the right, some stumbling and one man pausing long enough to throw up the contents of his dinner along the curb as they fled.

Leira pulled in energy as the symbols lit up along her

skin, flipping over at an ever increasing rate. Correk glanced down to get a glimpse of what the magic was predicting and grimaced. He didn't like what he saw.

As they got closer Leira formed a fireball in her hands, ready to aim it at whoever or whatever she saw first. At last she got to the side street set among three story brick buildings that must have looked picturesque in better times. But tonight, all Leira could focus on were the shifters growling and pawing at the ground on one side and the Witches and Wizards on the other in close quarters, their wands drawn. Trapped to one side, pinned against a dead end were the PDF agents, or what was left of them. Two were already laying still on the ground.

"Alan…" Leira watched in horror as Alan Cohen moved his gun back and forth between the two sides. He had the same determined look as when he faced down the dark mist.

Correk pulled out an arrow, lighting up the sharp end with a fireball and taking aim at Sirius Pickering standing in the front of the Wizards and Witches.

"Look out!" Agnes swung around with her wand, aiming it right at the arrow but not soon enough to deflect it entirely. The fiery ball caught Sirius in the shoulder, burning a hole through to the bone as he cried out in pain, dropping his wand. He gritted his teeth and picked up his wand with his other hand as he aimed it at the agent standing next to Alan.

Alan fired his gun, but this time Agnes did a better job of deflecting the bullet, creating a transparent shield of energy, sending the bullet around in a ricochet as Sirius sucked the breath out of another agent, dropping her to the cobblestone street, lifeless. Alan made himself stand still and fire again, putting himself between the dark magic and the two remaining agents behind him as the shifters closed in toward them.

Leira threw the fireball in her hand, watching it divide into a hundred smaller balls of blue fire, seeking out their targets, pelting the faces of the dark families standing in the front. The embers hit their targets, burning holes into their skin, not letting up as Leira ran as fast as she could toward the middle, feeling the muscles in her legs responding as she picked up speed.

The shifters growled, pawing the ground and moved in closer toward the agents.

Correk drew another arrow and aimed it at the shifters as Leira yelled to him. "Stop! They're not attacking the agents. Something is off. Where's Lucius? Aim at the families. Yumfuck defend the humans. I'm going to find Lucius. He's here somewhere."

Yumfuck turned his back to Correk, roaring at the shifters, swiping at the closest beast leaving a long thin wound along the shifter's neck and face. Correk stood directly behind him facing the dark families, his bow raised with another arrow, his jaw set. He aimed the arrow high over the heads of the front row at the Wizards and Witches behind them, showering them with blue embers, setting them on fire as they rolled on the ground, screaming. As he hoped, some of the front line turned with their wands to put out the flames and Correk saw his chance, firing off one arrow after another, all aimed at Sirius. *Take out the head of the snake.*

Alan stood his ground just to the right of Correk, still

aiming his gun, not sure what else to do. The remaining two agents behind him aimed their weapons at the shifters, their eyes wide with fear, even as they didn't give any ground. A shifter leapt at an agent as Yumfuck moved swiftly, catching the beast in the air and whipping him against the nearest brick wall, knocking him unconscious. He quickly shifted back to his human form, laying still on the ground.

The agents looked on in horror as they realized the beasts in front of them were part human. "What the fuck is going on?"

Sirius screamed in anger. His entire plan was blowing up in his face. None of his precious shifters were obeying his commands. Even the ones created from his own former ranks were siding with their alpha. Lucius.

CHAPTER THIRTY-FOUR

Leira moved down a side alley, sending out a stream of magic ahead of her. Find Lucius. She traced the stream of dark magic to an old patisserie. The front window was shattered and the bakers in dusty grey aprons were spilling out the front. *Found him.*

She rushed inside, running to the back and found herself face to face with Lucius, his claws wrapped tightly around Tess' arm, her long white hair falling across her face. Her eyes were a blank stare. An older baker with red hair was standing in front of Lucius, holding a long wooden peel, swatting at the beast as if he were just a pesky fly. A cigarette was firmly clamped in his mouth, smoke pouring out as his breathing picked up, determined to defend the seer from all comers. He wasn't going to betray his promise.

Leira threw a fireball at Lucius, watching it split into fragments as it found its target, as Lucius raised a claw to shred the lone baker. Leira sent out a pulse of energy, throwing the baker off his feet and out of harm's way just as the claws came down, barely missing their mark. Now it was between Leira and Lucius and the prize was the seer.

Tess raised her head and turned her face to the left and the right, sensing Leira's presence. "No…" she hissed. "This was the trap. Run! Get out! Run!"

Leira noticed too late. The black mist swept in, rolling in large clouds along the floor, already engulfing her legs. It had grown more powerful since Lucius had escaped the world in between. Leira could feel the cries of all the beings the dark mist had trapped. The sound was excruciating.

Lucius smiled, letting out a low growl. "I made a deal with the dark energy that runs through the void. My part of it was to deliver you. Getting Tess is a bonus," he growled.

Leira reached for the bracelet, taking it off her wrist, ready to fling it in Lucius' face. "Stop!" yelled Tess, reading the energy in front of her. "Just run!"

"I never run from a fight," whispered Leira as she raised her hand.

Something powerful shoved her back before she could throw the artifact, knocking her to the ground. She looked up to see Rhazdon standing in front of her, hunched over, facing Lucius.

"It's me you want, motherfucker!" Rhazdon raised her arms, swirling the black mist around all of them as if they were inside of a tornado, the familiar roar of a train drowning out the fight from the street.

"This was the part of the deal I was after," yelled Lucius, loosening his grip on Tess.

Rhazdon raised her withered arms, drawing on as

much energy as she could through her dying body as she whispered an ancient dark spell. Leira got to her feet, ready to fight.

He can't breathe. She's sucking the life out of him. Leira hesitated, not sure who to trust as Lucius bore down, his face grimacing in pain as he struggled to close in on Rhazdon. He let go of Tess as Leira reached out her hand, yanking at Tess' arm and pulling her close.

Lucius reared back, his mouth opened wide, screaming in pain as he decided to inflict a little pain of his own, grasping at Tess, scraping his claws along her arm. Leira grabbed onto Lucius' arm, the artifact still in her hand burning brightly, branding him with the liquid stone. The shifter yelped in pain, pulling back his hand as Rhazdon continued the spell.

But Lucius wasn't done, yet. He had waited eight hundred years for his revenge, always watching life moving on without him. He wasn't going to be denied. With his last breath, he lunged forward using the weight of his body to propel him the last of the way, sinking his claws into Rhazdon's chest, even as she whispered the last of the spell. There was a satisfying smile on his face as he collapsed to the ground, pushing deeper into her flesh, even as his body was shifting back into the form of a Light Elf.

Leira ran over to Rhazdon, even as the dark mist was creeping back toward her, this time more slowly. Leira grabbed towels from the counter and pressing them against Rhazdon's wound, watching the white linen turn a rapid crimson. "I can't stop it. Tell me how to stop it. You have to have a spell for this too."

Rhazdon looked up at Leira, locking eyes with her only inches apart. Her body was growing limp as she shifted one last time back to the beauty she had been all those years. She was young again, for just a moment.

"I'm sorry," she said, as she drew her last breath, gasping as the life ran out of her and her body quickly turned to ash, running through Leira's hands, sinking into the mist as it continued to rise, pulling at Leira's feet. Leira shook her head, anger and remorse coursing through her.

She stood upright, pulling in all the energy she could, dropping the bracelet as the light quickly spread through her, balancing out the darkness, opening up the void. Leira's eyes widened as she looked directly into the world in between and saw thousands of desperate faces looking back at her.

"Leira, no..." She looked toward the door in time to see Correk rushing in, Perrom and Ossonia right behind him.

"I'm sorry," she said, her eyes shining as she looked at Correk and the mist pulled her closer toward the edge. Correk reached for her hand, unwilling to let her go as Perrom held him back, using the energy of his bionic arm to stop his friend. Leira smiled for a moment at Perrom, grateful Correk was out of harm's way, even as the tips of her shoes went over the edge.

Ossonia saw an opening and slipped past Perrom and Correk, pulling in her own energy to shove Leira back just as the void opened wide, sucking her inside of the darkness as it closed around Ossonia's surprised face. Leira's eyes widened in horror and she summoned the energy within her, willing it to tear the void open again, the energy lifting her off the floor. But Leira could already feel the absence of the dark magic. The world in between was closed and with Ossonia inside of it even as the light sought to claim her for its own.

Perrom dropped his grip on Correk and screamed out, swiping at the air where Ossonia had just been standing, helpless to save her.

Correk slid across the floor, grabbing the artifact as the light continued to build in Leira, lifting her higher. He pulled her down closer to the ground, the bracelet digging in against her exposed stomach, all the while pulling her body toward him, pressing his chest tightly to her as the light did its best to push away the energy that sought to control it.

Every muscle in his body was at the breaking point as he held onto Leira, refusing to let go, the stone in the middle of the artifact spinning as it turned to liquid, pummeling back against the light.

The baker crawled in front of Tess, pushing her toward the secret passageway behind the enchanted oven. "Hniga dyrr soemiligr landi." The old door creaked open as the baker helped Tess to her feet and picked her up, carrying her down the stone steps of the kemana as the oven closed behind them. He had kept his word, his cigarette still clenched in his mouth.

The light began to give way, even as the energy still pulled through the middle of Leira, her toes still off the ground, burning through the scar on her abdomen. Correk held on tightly, unwilling to let go, the artifact pressed between them, his face inches from Leira's.

Leira grabbed onto him, wrapping her arms around his neck, pressing the side of her face against his, her fingers gripping his skin as the energy finally ebbed and the room grew quiet.

Leira's feet came down to the floor as Correk slipped the bracelet back on her wrist. "Never again. Make that another one of your rules."

"The agents..." Leira ducked around Correk, her arms slipping from around his neck as he tried to stop her.

"Don't Leira, it's over. The dark families are gone, and the shifters ran off." *You don't want to see what remains.* He left the rest unsaid, reaching out to grab her arm.

But she was already halfway out the door even as Correk turned back to his grieving friend.

"Ossonia! Ossonia!" Perrom was still screaming her name as if he would get an answer.

"We'll find a way to get her out. I promise you."

Leira ran down the side alley, listening for any signs of a battle or a wounded survivor, her heart pounding in the eerie silence. She ran into the space between the buildings and found the alpha shifter standing guard next to a fallen body.

Leira instinctively formed a fireball in her hand, ready to throw it as the alpha turned and looked at her.

"It's you."

The purple energy glowed in the palm of her hand. The shifter backed away from the body, lowering his head. "You're protecting him..." Leira let the flame die out and she saw who was lying there. "Alan... no..."

The alpha backed away further, turning to watch the

street as Leira ran to Alan, pressing her fingers against his neck. Still alive. There was a burn mark down his chest from a Wizard and he was still gripping his gun. Leira picked up his head and rested it in her lap.

"Alan, hang in there. Help is coming. Hang in there."

He opened his eyes and tried to smile at Leira as small red bubbles formed on his lips. "Leira." His voice came out in a throttled gurgle as she tried to surround them both in energy, but nothing was working.

"Alan, please, hang in there."

His eyelids fluttered as he raised a hand and touched her face, letting it drop to his chest and breathed his last. Leira ran her hands over his chest and face, trying to bring him back but it was too late. It was only then that she looked up and realized they were all dead. None of the agents had survived the attack. "The war has begun. It's too late to stop it now."

Yumfuck came running down the street, out of breath as Leira sat back, still holding onto Alan. He came to rest by her side, still eight feet tall, protecting Leira as Correk took his place by her side. Eventually, General Anderson arrived and the street quickly filled with other agents, reclaiming the dead.

Somewhere in the middle of the chaos, Lucius slipped away, freed from the curse but still a shifter, looking for his pack.

CHAPTER THIRTY-FIVE

Leira sat in the large room of the Garden Grove ranch in Buda, watching her grandmother fuss over her mother who was dressed in a long, cream colored wedding dress and a ring of roses atop her head. They were in a large villa getting ready for Eireka's wedding to Don, at last.

Two weeks had passed since the battle on the streets of Paris and Leira was still numb from the losses. She was grateful to have Correk next to her when she tried to sleep, jerking away in the night, replaying the last moments as she curled up next to him, feeling his even breaths next to her. She tried not to think of Perrom's anguished face as his father came to take his son home. Perrom looked up at Leira as he stepped through the portal and she reached out to him, but he turned away in pain.

"It's not your fault, Leira." Correk wrapped his arm around her, grateful she was safe, even as he mourned for Ossonia and Perrom, swallowing hard to hold back his grief.

General Anderson had cleaned up the streets and sent out a press release about terrorists and heavy losses, suppressing any reports of crazed wolves or strange beings with wands. But this time the rumors persisted despite his efforts.

Still, he had ordered Leira to say nothing.

Alan Cohen and his team were given medals posthumously that would be buried with each of them in order to keep the secrets. After their hastily arranged funeral, Leira turned in her resignation. In the end, Hagan did the same, settling in at the sanctuary and volunteering his services to Leira if she ever needed them.

"Once a partner, always a partner," he had said, gently patting her shoulder.

Still, today was her mother's wedding day and she had managed to keep the news from her all this time. She was determined not to slip now. *Let her have this day.* Leira took a deep breath and smiled at her mother. It was easy to do. Eireka Berens was so happy, turning around in her dress and touching the roses in her hair, the engagement ring sparkling in the light.

"I'm so glad the two of you are walking me down the aisle. It's just perfect." Eireka's joy was bubbling over. "Look, even your father sent a gift." Eireka held out a pale blue finely woven handkerchief with an embroidered B on it. "The note said it's an artifact that brings joy to the one who holds it. It's my something old."

"Oh, thank you. I was a little concerned that was going to be my role." Mara winked at her daughter as Eireka let out an easy laugh.

Leira smiled and stood up, silently thanking her dad. *I*

will need to go see him soon. Maybe I can tell him everything that's happened. "I'll be right back."

Mara looked over at Leira, her eyes narrowing as she studied her granddaughter, but she said nothing, instead smiling at her daughter and taking her hand.

Leira found her way outside and went out to the lawn where the guests were waiting, their chairs all turned toward the trellis at the end of the aisle, covered in vines and long, billowing white curtains draped on the sides. Leira stood back in the shadows and pulled in the energy from the ground, grateful to be using it for something to make someone she loved happy. She set out an intention and smiled as small blooms appeared on the vines and the scent of lilacs wafted across the grounds. The air glittered with flecks of gold in the sunlight as the guests all felt a lightness of being and couples reached out for each other's hand and friends smiled and laughed.

Leira made her way back to the room and held open the door. "It's time, Mom. You look beautiful, even radiant. I don't know that I've ever seen you this happy."

Eireka Berens stepped down from the small platform she had been standing on in front of the full-length mirrors and held out her arms, bent at the elbows. Mara put her hand through one side as Leira came and did the same on the other and the three Berens women made their way outside, together.

They paused at the back of the aisle, waiting for the music to start and everyone to stand. Leira took the bouquets from the wedding planner and handed the smaller one made of magnolias to her grandmother, and the larger one with trailing green vines to her mother, keeping another smaller one and holding it in front of her waist.

"Ready?" She looked at her mother, who smiled and kissed her daughter on her cheek. Eireka nodded and Leira gave her arm a gentle squeeze as they set off down the aisle. Toni and Jack were seated together, and Turner Underwood was right next to them. All of the regulars were bunched up near the front, waving and cheering, just like they had done at the bar for years. Estelle sat on the aisle, an unlit cigarette dangling in her mouth as she dabbed at her eyes with a tissue.

Leira saw Correk, standing tall in the front next to Don, dressed in a black tuxedo, his long silver hair hanging down past his shoulders. She smiled at him as Mara looked between the two of them and leaned across her daughter to whisper. "Well, it's about time."

Eireka looked up, surprised and smiled, crinkling her chin. "Thank goodness. I thought you two would never catch on."

Leira felt her face warm and whispered out the side of her mouth. "Today is all about you, Mom."

"When you're a parent it's never completely about you. You'll see some day."

"Okay, enough, we're almost to your groom. Be the bride for now."

They got to the top of the aisle and Leira and Mara took turns hugging Don and Eireka as they stepped back. Leira went and stood next to Correk, taking his hand, grateful he was there. He squeezed her hand and she felt the comfort of his energy surrounding her as she watched Eireka and Don exchange their vows. *My family grows a little bigger today. Despite everything, this is another good day. I can take this in.*

Correk leaned over and whispered, "Where's Yumfuck?"

Leira smiled, letting out a laugh. "He said he had something he needed to do for Mom. I suppose we'll find out what that means soon enough."

The minister looked up and held his arms out wide, smiling. "I now pronounce you husband and wife. You may kiss your bride."

Don dipped Eireka backward and said, "I've waited a very long time to be able to do this." He kissed his new wife as the crowd cheered and Leira's last surprise rose out of all the bushes. Hundreds of butterflies took flight, rising in the sunlight and hovering for a moment over the wedding as the guests looked up in surprise, gasping in amazement. Two white doves came and settled on the front of the trellis, letting out soft coos as the bride and groom, smiled and ran down the aisle, clutching each other's hand.

Don and Eireka waited till all the guests were gone before stepping through a portal to the sanctuary in Oriceran to spend their honeymoon. The Gardener of the Dark Forest had set up a cottage deep in the wood away from anything else. Yumfuck had gone ahead and spread the word among all his thousands of siblings and cousins and other related trolls, and they had gotten to work covering the cottage in flowers and lighting the roof with small orbs of light that floated just above the cottage in the moonlight.

The newly married couple stood at the doorway, shaking as many of the little paws as they could before Yumfuck smiled and waved to his family, signaling it was time to leave. Eireka and Don watched as the trolls quickly faded into the darkness, singing as they went, filling the air with music as they closed the door gently behind them.

Mara sat outside on the grounds of the twelve-acre ranch looking out over the hill country of Texas. She had taken off her shoes and her feet were propped up in a chair. Correk had gone inside to gather up their things as Leira took a seat next to her grandmother.

Mara reached out and took her granddaughter's hand and squeezed it tight, holding her hand to her chest. "Someday you will tell me what has put such sadness in your eyes, even as you have found such joy. It's okay, you don't need to protest. I know how you hate to lie, so I won't press you. You'll tell me when you're ready and I'll listen. Like I've always done for you. You know, I watched over you the best I could, even when I was trapped in that ugly place."

Leira winced thinking of Ossonia and looking around, wondering if the Light Elf who saved her could see her now. She swallowed hard, digging her nails into her palm. Mara noticed and reached over to open Leira's hand. "Do your best not to waste the precious time you have with regrets. It helps no one. If you have to make an amends about something, do it by the way you live your life. Make it count, be happy, choose for yourself the way it should look. Trust me, I plan to do the same."

"I think I can do that. I love you, Nana."

"I know you do, child. I'm going to get going. I'm leaving for Virginia in the morning. Time for a new adventure of my own. Turner Underwood's school is getting ready to open and I want to be there when it does. After all, I'll be the new headmistress."

"I would have thought parenting me would have knocked the idea of raising a few dozen more right out of you."

Mara let out a hoot of laughter and stood up. "Quite the opposite. You have always been the light of my life, along with your mother. I wouldn't have traded this adventure for anything. Even the bad parts because they all got me to this day. Come here and hug your Nana and promise to visit me often. You'll love Charlottesville. I'll teach you how to ride a horse."

"No thank you on the horses, but yes on the visits. Thank you for loving me and always setting such a kickass example. You're not the typical grandmother, you know."

"I'm a lot like you, Leira. Full of spit and vinegar mixed with magic. You'll see that life still has a lot of good in store for you, even as things turn darker. I know some of what happened in Paris."

Leira looked down at the ground, shutting her eyes and pressing her hand to her chest.

"Rumors like that travel fast through the magical community. Can't be sure what's fact and what's fiction, but it doesn't matter. What's clear is that the tipping point has been reached. Times have changed. Be careful out there while you try to hold the world together."

"I'm not trying to do that. Just do some good when I can with a swearing troll by my side."

"And a hunky Light Elf."

"That too."

"Smart girl. Go give 'em hell, Leira Berens. Let them know there's hell to be paid."

In full.

CHAPTER THIRTY-SIX

"Is that everything?" Leira looked back at the open door of the guest house. Correk was walking by her with the last of the boxes to the waiting U-Haul parked just in front of the bar. Her magic with parking spots was holding up for one more day. The troll was riding along in Correk's pocket, wrapped in a new pair of blue panties for the road and the green Mustang was loaded down with snacks for the road trip. Everything was ready.

"That's the last of it. Yumfuck and I will be at the car. You go say goodbye to the guest house." He smiled as he turned and walked toward the gate on the side of the yard. Estelle watched from behind the bar and waved at Correk as he left, a swirl of smoke around her head.

Leira walked into the guest house and shut the door quietly behind her, standing in the room with the old couch that would still be here if she needed it. The red velvet chair was safely tucked in the U-Haul and was going with them.

"Thank you for being here for me. Thank you for all the

memories you gave me." She walked to the window and looked out the blinds at the regulars lined up at the bar. They had all already said their goodbyes at a dinner last night. Leira had Estelle's brisket one last time and had listened as first Michael and then Paul, and Cassidy and Mitzi each made long toasts.

Leira had gotten up and raised her glass to them all. "Thank you for being my family when I didn't think I had one at all. I love each and every one of you and will take that love with me."

Leira turned around and walked through each room, saying goodbye as she walked out the door, leaving it ajar.

"Leira!" A cheer went up from the regulars as Estelle shrugged and let them do it, one last time. She poured a draft and set it down in front of Craig, waving to Leira as she left by the side gate, shutting it behind her.

Leira settled down in the front seat as the troll was busy pulling open the bag of Doritos. "You know the rules," said Leira. "Not till we're past the city limits. We have hours of driving ahead of us before we stop for the night."

Yumfuck looked up and smiled at Leira as he ran a sharp claw down the side, opening a slit in the bag, carefully reaching in and pulling out a chip, sliding it into his open mouth.

"Fuck it, you're right. New rules apply. We set our own course now." Leira started the car and pulled out into traffic. "No more trying to do what everyone else thinks is right."

"We'll figure it out as we go." Correk cracked the window and sat back. "I told Turner I was setting out on my own as the Fixer."

Leira looked over at Correk. "How'd he take that?"

"He said it was time. Every Fixer makes their own break and eventually has to find their own way."

"Louie is already in Georgetown, setting up the command center. He said the equipment was cutting edge. I made him swear he wouldn't sell off parts of it."

"I have to help Perrom."

"I know and we will, together. We got someone out of the world in between before. We'll find a way to do it again."

"The dark families are not going to give up, either, especially since their project turned on them. And Lucius is still out there."

"Correk, there's time. We'll face all of it and figure out the rules as we go."

"We will defend magic."

"Till we get it right." Leira drove past the sign, marking the border of Travis County and blew the horn, opening her window and yelling as loud as she could. "Aloha motherfuckers, it's been real!" She put her arm out the window, making the UT sign for hook 'em horns as Yumfuck pulled open the Twizzlers, biting off the end. "Yum... fuck..."

"Road trip!" Correk let out a loud whoop and settled back for the long ride, wondering just what awaited them. *The world has changed. I hope we're ready for it.*

The story is far from over. Leira's adventure continues in *DEFENDER OF MAGIC*!

Get sneak peeks, exclusive giveaways, behind the scenes content, and more. PLUS you'll be notified of special **one day only fan pricing** on new releases.

Sign up today to get free stories.

Visit: https://marthacarr.com/read-free-stories/

AUTHOR NOTES - MARTHA CARR

UPDATED JULY 3, 2020

We've made it to the fourth of July weekend, 2020. Nothing is so-called normal. People have asked me with a wry chuckle what I plan to do this weekend. To put it in perspective – I'm in Austin, Texas, and for now we're a hotbed of Covid-19.

But, life goes on and we still have to find joy, well, I do at least. That has set me on a daily search for gratitude and some days it's a snap. I'm in a great house, I have a lot of great books to write, there are great people to zoom with and long walks with the dogs.

Other days I have to look a little harder. Lately, it's been a bit harder. Like gear grinding harder. But a friend reminded me of a few things that didn't necessarily tell me what's coming next but still made it okay. She started with - I don't need to lean forward making my point to make sure I get what's mine or that I'm heard.

That's exhausting, anyway and what am I trying to prove and to who? Either I know what I'm worth and what's important or it doesn't matter. Those aren't things you can find from someone else anyway. And if that's where I'm looking, it means my worth will go up and down like a seesaw. Bad idea all around.

Instead, I can lean back and trust that the universe has my back - and in that space that gets created – that's where the real magic happens. Takes some courage and even more important, a tribe around me who run toward possibilities, not problems, but it's always doable to create that space.

And last part is to remember what really matters. It's not what I do, it's who I am and who is around me. (Okay, and a few good books and a couple of dogs). More adventures to follow.

Original: April 10, 2018

Okay, where to begin. I'm right in the middle of selling a house and buying/building a house. It's going better than can be expected and I hope to never do it again. A scootch stressful. The new house is bigger, beautiful and has a really amazing office and is close to downtown Austin. In other words, my own little slice of heaven. That's what happens when good starts rolling your way. Things change... for the better. Still feels like a roller coaster but I'm smart enough to not do it alone. Best part has been taking the ride (the books, the house...) with all of you celebrating right along with me!

And things are going to keep right on changing, including for Leira and company. If you've gotten this far, you know now that she's FINALLY hooked up with Correk, broken away from working for anyone and has said goodbye to her old life. Ready for the new one. And

Leira is doing it the way she does everything else – with open arms on her own terms and believing the solution is out there somewhere and she's going to find it.

Weird how my life is synced up with Leira's except for the fireballs and portals stuff.

So, what comes next... I'm starting two more series with Magic Mike this year – the first one is with Shay, a spinoff from his new series, *The Unbelievable Mr. Brownstone*. If you've read his first book, *Feared by Hell*, (and you should – a fast, fun ride) you know Shay is a hot, kickass tomb raider who's been known to solve her problems with a gun. The new series is called *I Fear No Evil* and Book One – *Kill the Willing*, will be out May 6th. And then... JUST ONE MORE! *The School of Necessary Magic*, which brings together Mara Berens and Allison from 'Brownstone' will start soon after that... Whew! The Oriceran Universe comes together – 20 years after Leira.

So, if you're keeping track. It's one dream house in a dream location, and 24 new books with my fave collaborator who helped change my life just because I was the one who stuck around – yeah, that guy... Michael Anderle. I'm telling you, it's been one helluva ride with more adventures to follow. Now if I can find my own Correk... Hell, every other dream has come true.

Still planning to hit the road some time this summer after I've moved, and visit fans across the country, as well as throwing a few more open houses for our Veterans and Fans. And hang out with the good dog, Lois Lane and the Offspring and the wonderful Katie. It's a great life and a lot of it is because all of you. Thank you Forever! Buckle Up People!

AUTHOR NOTES - MICHAEL ANDERLE

UPDATED JULY 28, 2020

It is with a touch of pride that I am writing these author notes the night BEFORE the updated version of this book goes live.

Why pride? Because I'm OG... I'm still working on my stuff last minute, and Martha has lapped me. She writes her stuff early, lays back, sipping tea with one eyebrow raised and a smirk on her face as I type my little fingers off to get these author notes done in time.

Frankly, she has it right. However, to assuage my little ego and what is left of my pride, allow me to pretend it's OG and cool to still do it old school.

Pretty please?

We hope you enjoyed the Director's Cut of the Leira Chronicles and are ready for some new books coming at ya!

Original: April 11, 2018

This is my salutation and appreciation for not only

reading through our story, but reading through our author notes as well!

Martha has provided some info about what is happening next, so I will give you a little background on how these stories came to be.

One year ago, I wanted to start a separate series called *The Unbelievable Mr. Brownstone*. I called Martha, she heard I wanted to start a universe, and Oriceran was born.

Our first Leira book came out on July 31, 2017 exactly one (1) year after she came to a meeting in Austin where I was speaking. Many collaborations and authors later a whole universe has been built, and provides stories about different aspects of Oriceran, Earth, and our joint history.

However, there haven't been any other stories besides Martha's that focus on Earth, the place I wanted to visit.

My original very short scene (seen in the beginning of the book, *Feared by Hell, The Unbelievable Mr. Brownstone*) was waiting for me to get back to it. However, I needed to finish my Paranormal Space Opera *The Kurtherian Gambit,* and so it took until April 6, 2018 for me to finally release my first Oriceran book.

It was my turn to put into the Oriceran Universe the grit I enjoy in the urban fantasy stories I like to read. I had no idea if the story would resonate or fall flat on its face.

I needed the world to be different than the existing timeline stories. We didn't talk about bounty hunters like the one in my story, so I had to jump some time. Martha and I elected to go forward twenty years.

I like my characters to have each other's backs, but there is a lot of room to see why there could be some friction between them.

Enter Shay... A woman with a past she doesn't want to divulge working with a man who upsets her world view, making her think twice about herself. She goes so far as to convince herself that Brownstone has a certain sexual preference so that her world view is safe.

Regardless of what Brownstone feels about her beliefs.

It ended up to be a great ass-kicking series that will make you smile and at times cry, "Oh, Shay, *NO!*" (Or perhaps, "Oh, Brownstone, *NO!*")

I HAVE TO TOUCH THE UPGRADES

Martha sent me a picture of her house that was still under construction last week. Along with that, she tells me every few days, "You are going to have to touch every upgrade when you come visit the first time."

I am a little creeped out.

I mean, *every* upgrade? I'd understand if she told me she wanted to *show* me every upgrade, because that makes sense. I'd want to be the proud papa of a new home and show my parents or friends everything we did with the house.

But touch it?

I think Martha is fucking with me, but I can't be sure. She is crafty; that "Aw shucks" exterior hides a devious mind. Yeah, that must be it. She is fucking with me...

Isn't she?

DAMMIT, CARR!

Ad Aeternitatem,
Michael Anderle

DARK IS HER NATURE

For Hire: Teachers for special school in Virginia countryside.

Must be able to handle teenagers with special abilities.

Cannot be afraid to discipline werewolves, wizards, elves and other assorted hormonal teens.

Apply at the School of Necessary Magic.

AVAILABLE ON AMAZON RETAILERS

THE MAGIC COMPASS

If smart phones and GPS rule the world - why am I hunting a magic compass to save the planet?

Austin Detective Maggie Parker has seen some weird things in her day, but finding a surly gnome rooting through her garage beats all.

Her world is about to be turned upside down in a frantic search for 4 Elementals.

Each one has an artifact that can keep the Earth humming along, but they need her to unite them first.

Unless the forces against her get there first.

<u>**AVAILABLE ON AMAZON AND IN KINDLE UNLIMITED!**</u>

OTHER SERIES IN THE ORICERAN UNIVERSE

SOUL STONE MAGE

THE KACY CHRONICLES

MIDWEST MAGIC CHRONICLES

THE FAIRHAVEN CHRONICLES

I FEAR NO EVIL

THE DANIEL CODEX SERIES

SCHOOL OF NECESSARY MAGIC

SCHOOL OF NECESSARY MAGIC: RAINE CAMPBELL

ALISON BROWNSTONE

FEDERAL AGENTS OF MAGIC

SCIONS OF MAGIC

THE UNBELIEVABLE MR. BROWNSTONE

OTHER BOOKS BY JUDITH BERENS

OTHER BOOKS BY MARTHA CARR

JOIN THE ORICERAN UNIVERSE FAN GROUP ON FACEBOOK!

BOOKS BY MICHAEL ANDERLE

For a complete list of books by Michael Anderle, please visit:

www.lmbpn.com/ma-books/

CONNECT WITH THE AUTHORS

Martha Carr Social
Website:
http://www.marthacarr.com
Facebook:
https://www.facebook.com/groups/MarthaCarrFans/

Michael Anderle Social
Website:
http://www.lmbpn.com
Email List:
http://lmbpn.com/email/
Facebook
https://www.facebook.com/LMBPNPublishing

www.ingramcontent.com/pod-product-compliance
Lightning Source LLC
Chambersburg PA
CBHW031644100726
47898CB00006B/1972